Everly is a runner. In his case it's a necessity, since he's a griffin shifter, and selling him on the black market could earn someone a pretty penny. But Everly doesn't fancy being sold, so he heads to Rosewood when someone tries to catch him again.

Kyle is a protector, not a lawyer or a doctor like his mother wants him to be. That's why he signed up for the new security team his alpha put together. It's just his luck that he's the one who finds Everly when the man walks into pack territory.

It's not until later that they realize they're mates.

Everly wants Rosewood to become his home, but he's never had one, and there are still people after him. He's been dealing with this for the past ten years, and he doesn't need anyone to protect him.

Or maybe he does. Kyle wants Everly to stay, and Everly wants the same. Will they be able to make Rosewood safe for Everly and all the other rare shifters out there, or will they fail and lose each other?

Flawed Assumptions
Copyright © 2021 Catherine Lievens
ISBN: 978-1-4874-3412-0
Cover art by Angela Waters

Published by eXtasy Books Inc

Look for us online at:
www.eXtasybooks.com

FLAWED ASSUMPTIONS
LEGENDARY SHIFTERS 7

BY

CATHERINE LIEVENS

CHAPTER ONE

Everly threw a pair of jeans into his backpack. A noise just outside his door made him freeze, and he waited, praying they hadn't found him yet. He knew they were coming, but he didn't know when. He had to get out of his apartment before they got to it, and he was nearly packed. He just needed a few more minutes.

When nothing happened, he went back to packing. Just in case, he opened his laptop and pulled up the surveillance program. He'd placed cameras everywhere he could without anyone noticing just for this kind of situation.

He kept an eye on the screen as he finished pushing clothes into his backpack, then gathered anything he couldn't leave behind. It wasn't much, but then, since he'd expected something like this to happen, he'd planned.

He'd never had a lot of things, and they'd dwindled over the years. Now, it only took him a couple of backpacks to get out, and one of them was full of computer equipment. It wasn't much to call his, but he'd never needed much, and when you were a rare shifter, it was almost impossible to find a safe place to put down roots and call home.

An alarm started blaring on his computer. He jumped but didn't pause to check what was happening. He already knew. They'd found him, and his time was over.

He looked around one last time, making sure he wouldn't leave anything crucial or anything that would help the hunters find him. Once he was sure he'd taken everything, he grabbed his laptop, pushed it into his backpack, and hauled both of the bags onto his shoulders.

He was too late.

His front door slammed open, startling him. Since he already knew he wouldn't get out without fighting, he dropped his bags and shifted. He was going to miss that shirt, dammit.

The torn bits of clothes weren't even on the floor yet before he attacked the two men coming through. He flapped his wings, trying to make as little noise as possible so the neighbors wouldn't realize something was happening. There wasn't a lot of space in the apartment, but it was enough for him to be able to rear up on his back legs and hit the first man coming in with his front legs. His claws dug into the man's chest, making him scream.

So much for not making noise for the neighbors.

The first man dropped to the floor, but the second was already there, trying to get to Everly. The man didn't shift, so either he was human, or there was a reason for him not to. Everly didn't care. He snapped his beak forward, but he didn't catch the man, who danced out of the way. How did he think he was going to capture Everly like this? As long as Everly was in his griffin form, neither of these men would touch him.

But they couldn't be alone, which meant more men were coming, and that could become dangerous. Everly had to get out of here as soon as possible.

He was ready to bet this man wasn't used to fighting against griffins. Not many people were, considering how rare griffins were. If he was smart, he'd have studied Everly's animal form, but that didn't mean he was ready for it. Everly had to take advantage of that.

He twisted around, slamming his tail against the man, who stumbled and hit the wall. Everly was already turning around and snapping his beak. He caught the man's arm, and the man started screaming. Blood spurted in Everly's mouth, making him grimace. *This* was why he didn't like fighting.

He shook his head, wincing at the tearing sound. It would be a miracle if this man was able to use his arm after Everly was done with him. As always, Everly felt guilty, but it was either defending himself or allowing this guy to take him, and that wasn't something he was willing to let happen. He didn't want to be locked up and never see the light of day again. He might not know why these guys wanted him, but it couldn't be anything good.

It never was.

The man slumped against the wall and slid down. Everly took advantage of that, snatching both his backpacks in his beak, and launched himself toward the window. He should have thought about opening it, but since he hadn't, he threw himself through it, knowing the broken glass wouldn't hurt him. His fur was too thick.

As soon as he was out, he opened his wings and prayed no one would see him. Some humans knew about shifters, but he doubted his neighbors did, and he didn't want anyone to notice him.

He circled his building, looking down and trying to understand whether there were more people looking for him. He was ready to bet that was the case, and he wasn't planning to linger but he was curious. He needed his truck, which, thankfully, he'd parked far enough away that he could get there from the sky. Hopefully that would give him enough time to get away before those guys found him again. He had no doubt they would. They always did, which was why he was always on the run.

He didn't see anyone else in front of his building, but that didn't mean anything. After a few moments, he turned and headed toward his truck. He'd found the perfect place to park it, in an alley hardly anyone ever visited. That gave him privacy to land in the back of the truck, drop his bags, shift, and quickly take clothes out of one of the bags to put them on. Once he was done, he looked around, but just like he'd expected, no one had noticed anything. The alley was still deserted, and apart from the rats scurrying around, he couldn't hear a sound.

He climbed out of the back of the truck, snatched the keys and phone from the bag they were in, and climbed into the front. He was breathing hard, but he couldn't risk taking time to rest. First he needed to get out of here, and that was what he focused on.

He drove as normally as possible so no one would realize someone was hunting him. He wasn't anywhere close to his apartment, so hopefully, no one was still after him. That might not last for long, but it would be long enough to give him time to escape.

He only relaxed once he was halfway out of the city. That was when he started thinking about what he was going to do. More importantly, he needed to decide where he'd go, and he had no idea.

He tapped his fingertips on the steering wheel. He was used to moving around every few months because someone was always hunting him, but he was tired of it. He couldn't help thinking about the rare shifters he'd helped over the years and who had found a place to call home. He'd never believed he could have anything like that, but damn if he didn't want to. He couldn't choose his next home thinking about that, though, so instead, he thought about the places that would be safer for him.

He'd taken everything he'd need with him in his bags, but that didn't make him feel better. Nothing would, and he had to wrap his mind around that. This was his life, and he needed to deal with it.

The problem was that he'd dealt with it for a long time, and it was starting to wear on him. When would people stop hunting him? When would he have a chance at a normal life?

He shook his head and turned on the stereo, hoping that some music would distract him. What he wanted or wished for didn't matter. The only thing that mattered was that he was safe and could continue helping the rare shifters around the country who contacted him through the network.

Maybe that was what he should do. He could contact someone from the network and ask them if they had a safe place for him to lay low, at least for a bit, until he decided where he wanted to stay next. Although he trusted Arvin, he didn't know if he trusted anyone else on the network, not with his life. He did with other people's lives, but it wasn't the same.

Everly had amassed a lot of information about rare shifters over the years, and it would be a disaster if anyone got their hands on that information. It would be a disaster if anyone got their hands on *him*, which meant he had to be extremely careful. Still, there were a few people he trusted, and he might just have to contact them this time. Doing everything on his own didn't seem to be working anymore, and maybe it was time to change things up.

Kyle bounced his knee, then eyed the door, wondering if he could get out before his mother managed to stop him. He was pretty sure she'd hidden a lasso somewhere in the kitchen to wrangle him or one of his siblings back into the room if they tried running, though. That was precisely the kind of thing she'd do and the kind of thing Kyle's siblings had managed to escape from. Kyle hadn't just yet, but hopefully, he would soon.

The problem was that he still lived in his childhood bed-room. He was the only one of his siblings at home, since Melissa lived with her husband, Todd had his own home, and

Jarvis recently moved in with his mate. That left Kyle, and their mother had become even more controlling now that he was the only one under her roof. She wasn't going to like what he was about to tell her, which was why he'd waited for so long.

He couldn't anymore.

No matter how little he was looking forward to having her scream at him for ruining his life, he wasn't backing down. He was twenty-four. He was an adult, even though he still lived at home. He could make his own decisions when it came to his life, and he had.

"Is the table set?" his mother asked from the stove.

Kyle swallowed. "The only things missing are the napkins."

"Well, get them. Food is ready."

He obeyed, then went to call his father. He might as well tell both his parents together, and besides, he hoped his father's presence would make it easier for his mother to accept.

It was a nice dream, if anything.

They sat around the table. Kyle's mother served them. Kyle looked down at the food — roast, potatoes, and carrots — but he wasn't hungry. Any other day, he would have fallen on his dinner like a starving wolf, but today he could barely manage to swallow a piece of carrot before he couldn't anymore. He pushed the food around, waiting for the perfect moment to explain what he'd done.

There would be no perfect moment. That was one thing he'd come to realize as he waited to tell his parents, which meant he should just come out and say it, even though his mother was going to be pissed. She would be angry any way he told her about this.

"You know about the new security team Cam is putting together?" he asked, trying to sound casual.

His father nodded and smiled, but his mother huffed.

"How can we not? I can't believe we need a security team. It's ridiculous."

"We need it for the rare shifters who live with us." One of which was her son's boyfriend.

But Peregrine had stood up to her, and she didn't like that. She didn't like *Peregrine*, and she was always angry when anyone brought him or Jarvis up in conversation. Since Jarvis had left home, she and Jarvis had barely talked, and Kyle doubted things would become easier anytime soon.

His mother had never been an easy person to deal with. It was easy for him to ignore how she'd clearly had favorites when he was growing up, and Jarvis hadn't been one of them. She'd picked on Jarvis, and, as a result, Kyle and his siblings had, too. Kyle felt like he was the worst offender, mainly because the others had left home eventually, and their relationship with Jarvis had changed. Kyle hadn't even realized what his mother had pushed him to do as he grew up, not until recently. Now that he had, he was horrified, and he couldn't wait to get out of here.

His mouth was dry, so he took a sip of water.

"If they're so dangerous, they shouldn't live with us," his mother said.

"They're not dangerous. If anything, they're in danger."

"Then they shouldn't put the rest of us in danger. I don't see why I have to watch people in uniform walking around. Life here was so nice until Camden became alpha."

Kyle suspected that Cam's father would have done pretty much the same thing as his son. The man had been a good alpha, and Cam was, too. Kyle's mother would have found something else to bitch about if it hadn't been this.

But this wasn't why Kyle had asked if she knew about the team.

"Cam is a good alpha, and he's doing everything he can to protect every single pack member," he said.

"He wouldn't have to protect us this way if he weren't accepting so many new people into our pack. How can he trust any of them?"

"I'm sure he has his reasons." Kyle had met the new shifters, and he liked all of them. More importantly, they'd needed help and had found it with their pack. That was what being a pack was about. When you needed something, the pack stepped in and helped you.

Kyle was proud to have an alpha like Cam, which was one of the reasons he'd signed up for the team. His mother wouldn't understand that, no matter how much he tried to explain to her or how long he waited to tell her.

He licked his lips. "Well, he was looking for volunteers to train and be put on that security team. I signed up."

There was a moment of silence. Kyle expected his mother to explode, but instead, she calmly put down her fork. He knew this wasn't over, so he tensed and waited for her reaction.

"No," she said.

"What do you mean?"

"I won't have you put yourself in danger. Besides, you have to focus on college."

Kyle winced. "About that. I quit."

The silence was so deep that Kyle felt he could cut it with a fork, never mind a knife.

"What do you mean, you quit?" his mother asked slowly.

"Exactly that." Kyle sucked in a breath and decided just to say everything he needed to say. "I never liked college. I tried because I know you and Dad wanted me to go, but it's not working. I'm not interested in anything I'm learning there, but I *am* interested in protecting the pack. That's why I was so happy when Cam created this team. I'd already been planning on quitting college, and I decided this was the perfect opportunity. This way, I'll go straight from college to having a job."

And wasn't that something his mother should be happy about?

But Kyle's mother wasn't like most mothers. She wasn't happy that he had a job, especially not this kind of job.

"You're going to quit the team and go back to college," she said. "I won't allow my son to do this. You can do much better than being a security guard, and I won't have you ruin your life."

Kyle shook his head. He'd known this was how she'd react, so he'd prepared his arguments. "You're not listening to me. I *want* to be a security guard. I want to train and help protect the pack."

"You want to be a doctor."

"That's what *you* want, Mom. You didn't give me a choice when I finished high school, and you still aren't. Don't you want me to be happy?"

"You can be happy once you're a doctor."

She was never going to understand or accept this, was she? Kyle expected it, but it still hurt to have the proof in front of him. "Please. I don't want to lose you over this, but I'm twenty-four. I can choose how to live my life, and I decided to live it like this. I'm sorry you're disappointed. I never wanted to be a doctor, and I won't go back to college. I already signed up for the team, and I'll start soon."

"You can't," Kyle's mother snapped.

He looked at his father, hoping for help. His father didn't look as angry as his mother, but he shook his head. Whether that meant that Kyle should stop pushing his mom or that he should ignore her reaction, Kyle didn't know.

But no matter how his parents felt, Kyle had already made his decision, and he wasn't changing his mind.

He got to his feet. "I'm sorry you feel that way, and I hope that eventually you'll be able to accept that this is what I want."

"Where are you going?" his mother screeched when he stepped away from the table.

"I think both of us need some time to think and get over our anger."

"Come back here, Kyle. You live under my roof, and as long as you do, you'll do what I tell you to do."

But Kyle had had enough. He ignored her and walked through the back door. He'd already known his mother would try something like this, but it still hurt.

This entire situation hurt. He'd hoped against all hope that his mother would want the best for him, but instead, she wanted what *she* thought was best.

Once he was far enough away to be safe, Everly stopped for coffee. He'd left the city behind about half an hour ago, and as far as he could see, no one had followed him. He hoped he wasn't wrong, but if he was, he'd deal with it.

His coffee and a sandwich in hand, he went back to his truck. He didn't turn on the engine as soon as he was inside, though. He needed to do something first, and he was finally ready for it.

He put his sandwich on the passenger seat and took out his phone. Thankfully, he'd remembered to put it into his backpack rather than his pocket when he'd packed. If he hadn't, the phone would still be back at his apartment with his torn clothes, and he'd be in trouble.

He unlocked the phone, found the number he was looking for, and hit *call*.

It rang a few times before Arvin's voice came through. "Everly?"

Just like always, Everly relaxed at the sound of Arvin's voice. They'd never met, but he knew Arvin was older, and he felt almost like a grandfather to Everly. He'd never told Arvin that, but he suspected Arvin knew. He'd always treated Everly differently from anyone else in the network, more like family than someone they needed to work with to keep other people safe.

"Hi," Everly said breathlessly. His chest felt tight, and he wanted to cry.

He'd been on the run for what felt like his entire life, and really, that was almost the case. He'd started running when he was seventeen, and now that he was in his late twenties, he wanted it to stop. The problem was that considering what kind of shifter he was, it was impossible. Some rare shifters managed to find a place to call home, but Everly never had.

"What happened?" Arvin asked.

Obviously, he'd been able to read Everly's tone. Everly wasn't surprised. "I had to leave."

Arvin swore. "Who found you?"

"I didn't stick around to ask questions. Besides, I doubt either of the guys who came in my apartment would have answered, considering the state I left them in."

"Good boy. You're on the run?"

"Pretty much. I managed to grab my computer, so everyone on the network is safe."

"That's a good thing, but it's not what I'm worried about."

Everly found himself smiling. Arvin was worried about him as a person, not because he was the one who'd created the rare shifters network. That felt good, and it gave Everly hope.

Even if he never managed to call a place home, he'd always have this. He'd always have Arvin, and that was what he needed to focus on, not on what he kept losing every time he had to run.

"I'll be fine," he promised.

"I know you will, but you can't continue living like this.

You've been on the run for as long as I've known you."

"Not everyone is as lucky as you and your family."

Arvin was the alpha of his tiny pack of dire wolves. They'd had to run several times over the years, but now they'd found their place, and they'd settled down. He'd offered Everly a spot in his pack, but Everly didn't want to bring his problems to Arvin and his family. He'd never forgive himself if something happened to them because of him.

"You could be, but I already know what your answer will be. Besides, you're not wrong, as little as I like to admit it. There are so few of us that we wouldn't be able to protect you adequately. There might be the solution to this, though."

"As long as I'm not putting anyone in danger."

"You're always putting someone in danger, even when that someone is you. I think that the best thing you can do now is to go to Rosewood."

Everly knew about Rosewood and the pack that lived there. They'd become a legend over the network because of how many rare shifters had chosen Rosewood as their home. Everly didn't know the alpha personally, but he'd heard good things about him, and he couldn't deny the man was doing everything he could to protect the rare shifters who called Rosewood home.

"I can't do that to him and his people," Everly said.

"You wouldn't do anything to them. Camden would be more than happy to have you with them. He's a good person, and he's trying hard to protect his pack."

"That's why taking my problems there is the worst thing I can do."

"They're already in trouble. With so many rare shifters living there, Cam had to implement a new security team. He's looking into fencing pack territory, and he needs a security system. You're good with computers, so I'm sure you could help him there."

"I could, but would he be okay with that?"

"I'll call him and ask, but I'm pretty sure his answer will be yes. He knows how you've helped Peregrine and that I'm friends with you. Besides, if I tell him you could help with the security system, he'll jump on the opportunity. He's had to deal with a lot of hunted shifters in the recent past. He knows what he's up against, and he won't hesitate to help you. Look at it this way. If it weren't you, it would be someone else."

"Maybe it would be better for him not to have rare shifters in his pack," Everly murmured.

"Maybe so, but they're there to stay. His mate is a rare shifter. Cam will do the right thing when it comes to Toby and everyone else, including you."

Everly had no intention of continuing to say no. He needed a safe place to stay, and if he could get a job while laying low, all the better. Even if the alpha didn't pay him for the security system, as long as Everly had a roof over his head and food in his stomach, he'd be fine.

"And they have phoenixes," Arvin continued.

Everly laughed. "You know how to convince a man."

"I also know how fascinating you find phoenixes. I honestly don't understand it, but they're nice enough."

"One of those phoenixes is your grandson's mate," Everly pointed out.

"That's why I said they're nice enough. Lennox is great, but his brother is a bit strange."

From what Everly had heard about the twins, he knew what Arvin was talking about.

As much as he wanted to continue talking to his friend, he needed to get moving. "You'll let me know what Cam says?"

"I'll call him as soon as I hang up with you. I'll text you his answer so you don't have to answer another phone call, since I'm sure you're in your truck. He's going to say yes, though. He'd be a fool not to."

"Maybe he just doesn't want to add more trouble than he already has on his plate."

"Even if that's what he decides, you won't be alone. If the Rosewood pack can't welcome you, we will."

"Thank you."

Everly was touched, much more than he could put into words.

For most of his life, he'd been alone. He'd grown up in foster care, and when some guys had tried to kidnap him, he'd run. He'd known what they were trying to do and that it wouldn't end well for him if they caught him. That had happened when he was seventeen, and ever since, he hadn't allowed himself to care for anyone. He was a loner, both because he enjoyed his own company and out of necessity. He also didn't want to put anyone else in danger, but Arvin and his family understood, and even though Cam wasn't a rare shifter, he did, too.

Everly knew he wasn't finding a family or a home, not permanently, but that wasn't in his cards. The only thing he needed right now was a safe place to lay low for a while, and it looked like he'd found it.

Kyle didn't know where to go. He couldn't go home, not when he'd just left and his mother was still pissed. Of course that wouldn't change anytime soon, and eventually he'd have to go back. He'd face her when he was ready to, which wasn't now.

But that left him at a loss. He could go to Melissa and her husband, but as much as he liked them, he didn't want to intrude. Besides, their daughter would no doubt ask what he was doing there, and he didn't want to badmouth her grandmother, no matter how angry he was at his mother.

Maybe he could go to Todd's, but there was always a

chance of stumbling in on Todd with his latest flavor of the week, and that wasn't something Kyle wanted to deal with right now, either.

That left one of Kyle's grandparents, but he didn't want to pull them into the fight with his mother. Marcus, Kyle's best friend, wouldn't have a problem with him staying at his apartment, but he was still going to college, which meant he often had parties or one-night stands over.

Then there was Jarvis. He, better than anyone, would understand why Kyle wanted to stay away from their mother. The problem was that Kyle wasn't sure Jarvis would welcome him, and even if he did, whether Peregrine would agree to have Kyle stay over. Most of the time, it felt like Peregrine hated Kyle more than Jarvis did, which Kyle understood. Jarvis had always been too good, and it came down to Peregrine to protect his mate from his own family. He shouldn't have to, but as it was, Kyle was happy his brother had found someone to protect him.

It wasn't an easy choice, but Kyle headed over to Jarvis's house. Even if Peregrine refused to open the door, this felt like a good time to start making peace with Jarvis. Kyle had already apologized, but he didn't feel it had been enough. He wanted to show Jarvis he'd changed, and the only way to do that was to talk to him more than once.

The lights were on in the house when he got there. He could hear music and soft voices, and he hoped he wouldn't be interrupting anything. It was still strange to think about his brother having a mate, but he'd never seen Jarvis as happy as he was with Peregrine. Kyle wanted Jarvis to be happy, and he hated himself for what he'd done to his brother in the past.

He climbed the porch steps and knocked on the door, holding his breath as he waited for someone to answer. He almost groaned when he saw Peregrine, but Kyle had known he'd have to face the man sooner rather than later, and he supposed it might as well be now.

Peregrine blinked, then frowned. "Kyle."

Kyle forced himself to smile. "Hi. I hope I'm not bothering you?"

"I suppose it depends on why you're here. You want to talk to Jarvis?"

"Please."

Peregrine hesitated, and Kyle was surprised when he eventually stepped aside. "Jarvis is in the kitchen. I'm letting you in even though I don't want to."

"Thank you."

Kyle had no idea where the kitchen was, since he'd never been here, so he waited for Peregrine to close the door, then followed him deeper into the house. The music he'd heard from outside came from the kitchen, where his brother was dancing around as he cleaned up the dinner he and Peregrine had apparently just finished eating. He turned toward the door when he heard Peregrine and smiled, but his smile froze when he noticed Kyle standing there.

He stopped dancing, and while Kyle wanted to tell him he didn't have to, he kept his mouth shut. He was the reason Jarvis was uncomfortable around him, and it would take time to get over it for both of them.

"Hi," he said.

"What are you doing here?" Jarvis asked.

Kyle winced, but he didn't blame his brother for wanting to go right to the point.

Peregrine walked past Jarvis and patted his shoulder. "I'll make coffee, but don't drink too much of it, or you won't sleep tonight."

Jarvis's cheeks flushed, but he nodded. "I promise I won't." When he turned to Kyle again, he was smiling. "The last evening that I drank too much coffee, I couldn't sleep until four AM, and Peregrine wasn't happy."

"I remember you have trouble with caffeine," Kyle said.

Jarvis gestured at the table. "Why don't you sit down? I suppose you're here to talk about something?"

Kyle grimaced. "Not really. I'm running from Mom, and I didn't know where else to go."

Jarvis blinked. "And you could only think of me?"

"No, but you were my best option."

"I find that surprising."

Kyle sighed. "I wanted to see you. You better than anyone can understand why I left home."

"Is it temporary, or are you moving out?"

"I'm planning on moving out as soon as possible, but for now, it's only for tonight." Kyle hesitated, but he'd come here to talk, and his brother would find out about what he'd done anyway. "I told our parents that I quit college and signed up for the security team Cam is putting together."

Jarvis looked stunned for a moment before grimacing. "That would do it. I'm guessing Mom didn't take it well?"

"That's an understatement. She was *pissed.*"

"And now you're on the run. She's going to find you eventually."

"I wouldn't be surprised. I just need time, and I'm hoping that once she thinks about it, she'll accept it."

Peregrine snorted. "Even I know she won't, and I barely know her. I like you a bit more now that I know all of this, though."

Kyle found himself smiling. "That's good."

"What's good is that you're standing up to our mother," Jarvis intervened. "Honestly, I didn't think you had it in you."

"I'm sorry you have such a bad opinion of me, and I realize it's my fault, but I hope I'll be able to show you I'm better now."

Jarvis smiled and patted Kyle's hand. "I already know you are. You apologized, and while our relationship isn't what I want it to be, I know we'll work on it and fix it. But I know how hard it is to stand up to our mother, and I'm glad you did it. This has to be important to you."

"It is. I never wanted to be a doctor, but she never listened no matter how many times I told her that. You know how she is."

"I can remember all too easily," Jarvis said with a grimace. "She hit the roof when you told her, didn't she?"

"She was already saying things about rare shifters that I didn't like, and she didn't take it well when I said something about it. Telling her that I quit college was the straw that broke the camel's back. She also doesn't like that I signed up for the security team. She thinks I could do better." Kyle was bitter about that. He understood that every parent wanted their children to succeed, but success didn't mean being a doctor or a lawyer or earning a lot of money. Kyle had tried, but he just couldn't see himself as a doctor. He'd hated the classes he'd taken, and he suspected he would hate being a doctor just as much, if not more.

No, he'd done the right thing, getting out in time. He might lose his mother over it, but if that was what happened, well, he'd deal with it. Right now, it didn't feel like a great loss, although he knew the feeling would change. No matter how much he disliked his mother's behavior, she was still his mother.

"Well, you can stay here as long as you want," Jarvis said.

Kyle was surprised. "Why would you let me stay after the way I treated you?"

"That's all in the past. I know you're sorry and that you won't do it again. It's enough for me. You're my brother, and I'm glad to have you back in my life."

"But if you hurt him again, you'll have to answer to me," Peregrine said as he put down two cups of steaming coffee in front of them.

Even though he was threatening Kyle, Kyle found himself smiling. "I promise that if I hurt Jarvis again, you can have first go at me."

The smile Peregrine gave him was all teeth. "Glad I have your approval, but I didn't need it."

Kyle might have lost his parents, but he had his brother back, and in the end, that was all that mattered. He wouldn't allow his mother to reign over his life anymore. He'd allowed it for too long, and he'd almost lost Jarvis because of it.

He had no idea what his future would be like, but he wouldn't have been happy doing what his mother wanted. Hopefully, now that he was making his own choices, he would be.

CHAPTER TWO

Everly still believed this was a bad idea, but he couldn't think of an alternative. Arvin had confirmed he'd be welcome in Rosewood, so that was where Everly was headed. He hadn't noticed anyone following him, and he hoped that would continue. He had no intention of bringing danger to the Rosewood pack's doorstep, so if anyone tried coming after him, he'd have to find another place to stay. For now, though, Rosewood it was.

Everly couldn't say he was sorry. He'd been curious about Rosewood since he'd found out about the place, and he wanted to see it for himself. Most days, he had a hard time believing it truly was a safe haven that so many rare shifters had chosen as their home. There was no denying how many lived there, though. That was one of the reasons Everly was curious, but he also wanted to know the alpha. He was aware that Cam's mate was a rare shifter, but was that the only reason Cam was taking in so many rare shifters? Could he be such a generous man? And what about the rest of his pack? What did they think about being overrun with rare shifters and having to protect them?

Those thoughts swirled in Everly's mind as he drove toward Rosewood. Arvin had promised Rosewood would be safe for him, and he trusted Arvin. Besides, it would be nice not to have to look over his shoulder every single moment of every day. He had a hard time believing he really wouldn't have to in Rosewood, but he couldn't wait to find out.

It was a long way to Rosewood, and even though Everly

didn't like it, he'd have to stop. If anything, he needed a shower, and he needed it soon. He could smell himself, which meant things were bad.

He drove for as long as he could, spending part of the night on the roads. Once dawn peeked at the horizon, he found a motel and stopped. He didn't know if he'd be able to sleep, but at least he'd have warm water and a safe place to rest for a moment. He also wanted to call Arvin again. The other man had texted him to tell him Cam had said yes, and Everly wanted more details.

When he stepped inside the room, his first instinct was to throw himself onto the bed, but he knew better. If he did that before showering and calling Arvin, he'd waste a lot of time because he'd fall asleep instantly. It was tempting, but he needed to know where he stood before he could relax.

Instead of flopping onto the bed, he sat on its edge, ignoring the room around him. It was a typical motel room, albeit somewhat cleaner than what he was used to. He couldn't say he minded, even though he was surprised.

He took his phone out of his pocket and dialed Arvin's number. He only realized how early it was when Arvin answered in a gruff voice. "Everly? Everything okay?"

"Yes, sorry. I should have checked the time before calling," Everly apologized.

"Don't worry about it. I'm an old man, so I don't need as much sleep as I did when I was young."

"You're not old."

Arvin chuckled. "And how would you know that? You've never met me."

That much was true. "Well, you don't sound old."

"I suppose I should be grateful. But I *am* an older man, Everly. Remember that I have adult grandchildren."

Everly had never met any of them, but Arvin had told him plenty about them. Everly even knew about Owen, who'd been lost as a child and had only found his family recently. Arvin talked about them incessantly, and while some people would have found that annoying, Everly found it soothing. It made him feel like he was part of it, even though nothing was further from the truth.

"So, if you're not in trouble, why are you calling?" Arvin asked.

"I saw your text earlier about Cam allowing me to stay with the pack."

"And you wanted to confirm it before you arrived."

"I did. Not that I don't trust you, but I'd rather know what I'm about to face."

"You don't trust a lot of people."

"I don't, but I trust *you*. If you say I'll be safe in Rosewood, then I will. I just want to know a little bit more."

Arvin sighed.

Everly heard sounds as if Arvin was settling down, and he imagined that was the case. He really should have checked the time before calling.

"Well, there's not a lot you don't know about Rosewood. I'm sure you'll meet Cam and Toby, his mate."

"Who's a unicorn shifter."

"He is," Arvin confirmed. "He and his brother Sam were the first rare shifters to move in with the pack. Sam's mate is also a pack member."

"What other rare shifters are there now?"

"Let's see if I remember all of them. There's my grandson, of course, and his mate. Owen is a dire wolf, while Lennox is a phoenix. Lennox's twin brother lives there, too, along with both his boyfriends. Sage is a jackalope shifter. Then, of course, there's Peregrine, who you already know."

"So that's six, seven with me."

"Correct. I suppose seven people isn't a lot, but we're talking about rare shifters."

"It's a miracle the pack hasn't been attacked yet."

"Oh, they've had to deal with their share of problems. They contacted a few packs in the area for help, but I don't know how that's going. You'll have to ask Cam for more details."

"I will. Is there anything else I should know?"

Arvin hesitated, and Everly braced himself for bad news. It was nothing new, but sometimes, he wished he didn't have to expect it.

"I'd like it if you considered Rosewood as a place to settle down," Arvin finally said.

That wasn't what Everly had been expecting. "What do you mean?"

"I've never met you, but I know enough about you to be aware of the fact that you've been on the run most of your life. I understand the need for that more than many people could, but I also know no one is made for being on the run for so long. You shouldn't have to."

"I agree, but I don't see a solution. People are always going to hunt me and other rare shifters."

"Unfortunately, that's the truth. But you've been alone a long time, Everly. You've survived, but you haven't *lived*. Maybe it's time to find a place to call home, and I think Rosewood could be that for you. I know you can't make any promises, but I'd like it if you at least give Rosewood a chance."

Everly's first instinct was to say no. He couldn't afford to stay in one place for too long, not with people hunting him. But Peregrine and the others had settled down in Rosewood. It was dangerous, and if someone found out, they'd try to grab them, but that hadn't stopped Peregrine from finally claiming the life he'd never been allowed to have.

Everly knew some of Peregrine's story, so he was aware of the fact that much like him, Peregrine had been on the run since he was a teenager. He'd never had a place to put down roots until Rosewood, but now he had a home and a boyfriend, and the few times Everly had heard from him, he'd sounded happy.

Could Everly have that?

He wanted to think so, but he was also afraid to. He didn't want to hope, only to have those hopes torn apart when he faced reality.

He cleared his throat. "We'll see. I don't feel I can promise anything right now, not when I still haven't seen Rosewood."

"And I don't expect any promises. I just want you to give Rosewood a chance. If not Rosewood, my pack. I want to help you, Everly. I don't know about you, but I feel close to you after the many times we've talked on the phone, and I dislike the thought of you running all over the country, not when there's an alternative."

Everly wasn't sure there was. He wanted to believe so, but he'd thought he'd found his place in the world too many times, only to have hunters find him and destroy everything. The same would no doubt happen in Rosewood, no matter how much Everly wanted to believe that wouldn't be the case.

Kyle woke up early the following day. For a moment, he couldn't remember where he was. He was sure he'd never been in this room, but it didn't take him long to realize he hadn't.

He still had a hard time believing that Peregrine had allowed him to stay. He'd thought Jarvis's boyfriend would kick him out, but instead, he'd been welcoming, especially once Jarvis and Kyle had talked. It would take time for Kyle and Peregrine to become family, but Kyle felt they'd taken a step toward that. He hoped Peregrine felt the same because things would be awkward if he didn't.

He took a moment to listen to the sounds of the house. He couldn't hear anyone moving around, so he suspected Jarvis and Peregrine were still asleep, or in their bedroom, anyway. He didn't want to think about what his brother and Peregrine were up to in there. But then his thoughts drifted to his mother and what had happened yesterday, and that was even worse.

Kyle groaned and buried his face into his pillow.

Jarvis and Peregrine had told him he was welcome to stay with them for as long as he wanted, and he was tempted to accept the offer. On the other hand, he doubted they'd be happy if he stayed more than a few weeks, if even that. He realized they wanted to help him, and he was grateful, but he wasn't sure that moving in with them was the best idea.

Neither was going home.

His mother would pounce as soon as he stepped in through the door. After what she'd said yesterday, he had no doubt she'd use the *as long as you live under my roof* excuse, which meant Kyle needed to not live under her roof anymore. The easiest way to make that happen would be to ask Cam if he knew of someone looking for a roommate, but Kyle was wary of doing that. Cam already had enough trouble, as the security team he was putting together showed. He didn't need Kyle to add to it.

A soft knock at his door made him sit up. It could only be one of two people, and he doubted it was Peregrine. "Come in," he called out.

The door creaked open, and Jarvis's head appeared. "I wasn't sure you'd be awake."

"I didn't want to get up in case you and Peregrine were still sleeping. Do you want me to take care of breakfast?"

Jarvis waved away Kyle's offer. "We're already working on it. You should come to the kitchen once you're ready. We can have breakfast together and talk."

Because Kyle had to decide what he was going to do. He was excited about finally feeling like a grown-up, moving out of his childhood bedroom, and finding his place in the pack, but it was also terrifying. What if he sucked as an adult? What if he just couldn't do it and all of this ended up being a disaster? The last thing he wanted was to have to go back home with his tail between his legs, both literally and figuratively. His mother would be happy if that was what happened, but Kyle definitely wouldn't.

That meant he'd have to succeed at whatever was next for him.

He took a shower, even though he didn't have clean clothes to wear. He skipped the underwear, folding his boxer briefs and stuffing them into his jeans' pocket. He didn't particularly enjoy going commando, but it wasn't like he had a choice.

When he stepped out of the bedroom, he could smell breakfast in the air. He made his way to the kitchen, smiling when he heard Peregrine and Jarvis talking to each other. Their voices were soft, and he didn't think he'd ever heard Jarvis talk to anyone that way.

Jarvis had been lucky to meet his mate. Kyle had never quite thought about it, knowing he was too young to settle down, but maybe he wasn't. Jarvis was only a few years older, and he hadn't had a problem with moving in with Peregrine. He was happier than Kyle had ever seen him, and it made Kyle want the same thing for himself.

Maybe he would, one day. First, though, he needed to focus on solving the problems at hand, which meant finding a place to stay, and hopefully avoiding his mother for as long as possible.

Jarvis smiled when Kyle stepped into the kitchen. Peregrine was a bit more reserved, but he nodded, and even though things weren't okay between them yet, Kyle hoped they would be eventually. With Peregrine staying in Rosewood, Kyle had all the time in the world to show him how sorry he was for how he'd treated Jarvis.

"Did you sleep well?" Jarvis asked as they settled around the table.

"Better than I have in a long time."

"I think knowing you won't have to wake up at dawn to help Mom around the house helped," Jarvis said with a snicker.

"She forced you to wake up early?" Peregrine asked. He looked angry again, even though they were only talking about having to wake up early. He was protective of Jarvis, and it was good to see.

"It wasn't a bad thing," Jarvis reassured him. "It means that once I got a job, I didn't have a problem getting up on time, and besides, I didn't mind helping her around the house. It's just that I wish I could have slept in at least during the weekends, you know?"

"Well, you certainly do now."

"It's one of the perks of having your own place," Jarvis told Kyle. "I know it can be overwhelming to think about everything you have to do yourself once you live on your own, but I promise it's worth it. Besides, you need to put some distance between you and Mom. As long as you hesitate, she'll dig her claws in and try to pull you back."

"I won't let her," Kyle said after taking a sip of coffee. Today, more than ever, he was convinced of what he was doing. It was the right thing for him, and he wouldn't let anyone talk him out of it, especially not their mother.

Jarvis nodded and looked at Peregrine. Peregrine looked back the way some couples had of talking to each other without saying a word. They had what felt like an entire conversation before Jarvis turned to Kyle again. "Peregrine and I talked, and we haven't changed our minds. If you want to move in with us, you're welcome to do just that."

It was tempting. Jarvis's house would be a safe place for

Kyle, and they had the space. The house wasn't huge, but there was a guest room, and Kyle felt at home. He also enjoyed spending time with Jarvis and Peregrine, and he wanted to see more of his brother.

But accepting would be like going from one safe place to another, and it was time for Kyle to live his life. He couldn't always play it safe.

"I'm thankful for the offer," he started, trying to find the right words to say no without offending or angering Jarvis.

"But it's a no," Jarvis said with a smile.

"I want to say yes, but I feel like I need to start being on my own. It's what adults do."

"I can't say I disagree, but you're already going through a lot of changes. You left what's been your home your whole life, and you quit college. You're fighting with Mom. You have a new job. Do you want to add house hunting to that? Besides, unless you find a place in town, I don't know if there's much available here. Are there empty houses in pack territory?"

"I'd have to ask Cam."

"Then ask him about it," Peregrine said in a gruff voice. "But unless you want to keep living with your mother in the meantime, you should move in with us. It would only be temporary. It's not like I want you to move into my guest room permanently."

Kyle grinned. "I knew you loved me."

"I wouldn't go that far." Peregrine grinned back. "I tolerate you because of Jarvis, but that's about it. Stop obsessing over this and accept the offer. You'll make Jarvis happy."

And it would allow him to move away from his mother. As far as Kyle could see, it was a win-win situation.

Everly was almost in Rosewood. A few more miles, and he'd

be safe, or at least that was what he'd been telling himself. He truly hoped he *would* be safe, at least for a while.

Arvin was right. Everly had been on the run for most of his life, and it was starting to wear on him. It wasn't like he had a choice, or maybe he did.

He'd never considered staying in one place for long. It would have been stupid when he hadn't had help, but this time was different. This time, he'd have an entire pack protecting him, and maybe it finally was time to start to think about what was next for him. He couldn't continue running for the rest of his life, no matter how much his instinct told him that was what he needed to do. It was impractical, even when he didn't consider that he didn't have anyone in his life and that no one was made to be alone all the time.

Everly had always tried to keep people away so he wouldn't have to hurt them when the time came for him to run, or worse when some of the people hunting him found him. He would never have forgiven himself if someone had been hurt because of him, and he still wouldn't.

But maybe nothing would happen. Like Arvin and other rare shifters were showing, it was possible for them to find a place to call home, and while Everly still wasn't sure it was for him, maybe he should give it a try. He'd have to lay low in Rosewood for a while, anyway. He could give this a try, see what happened, and make a decision in a bit. Besides, he wasn't the only one involved. No matter how much he wanted to find a home, he might not find it in Rosewood.

When he finally saw the sign that welcomed him to Rosewood, he relaxed. It was still possible that someone was coming after him, but they hadn't tried to catch him since he left the city, so he doubted it. He'd still be careful, but then, he always was.

Arvin had sent Everly the coordinates of the Rosewood pack, and even though Everly wanted to stop in town and rest, he drove straight there. From what he'd gathered, most of Rosewood didn't know about shifters. Some people no doubt realized something was wrong with the people who lived with the pack, or maybe they thought it was a commune or something like that. Maybe some of the humans who lived in town and knew what shifters were didn't care.

There was no way for shifters to be entirely hidden. That meant that some humans were aware of their existence, and it had always surprised Everly that they didn't tell everything to the authorities right away or that they didn't try to take advantage of it. Some did, but Arvin hadn't said anything about the humans in Rosewood, so Everly thought it wouldn't be the case. He certainly hoped it wouldn't, because he couldn't deal with any more complications.

Everly slowed once he reached the coordinates Arvin had sent him, looking for a sign that he'd arrived in pack territory. He wasn't sure what to look for. He'd never lived with a pack, not even when he was a child.

He noticed a few houses in the distance. That had to be the pack, and he doubted they'd be happy if Everly just drove straight to the center. Everly had no idea how the pack was set up, so he decided to park his truck away from the houses and go the rest of the way on foot.

He breathed in once he was out of the truck, smiling at the scent of the forest. He'd never lived out in the country. It had been safer for him to stick to cities where he could blend in with thousands of other people, but this was going to be nice. He kind of hoped to be able to stay longer than he usually stayed in one place.

He locked the truck and looked around. There was no one to be seen, and he wasn't sure what to do. Should he just head toward the houses and hope for the best? Should he stay with his truck and wait for someone to realize he was here?

Since he didn't want to just hang around the forest by

himself like an idiot, he started walking toward the houses.

A branch cracked behind him. He froze, afraid to look back. Had the people after him found him? He hadn't thought it possible, but he should have known better. They always found him, no matter how far he ran.

There was more noise behind Everly, and he acted without thinking. He shifted, mourning the loss of a second change of clothes, and twirled to face his attacker.

A young man stood there, his eyes wide, his hands held up as if he were trying to show Everly he wasn't a danger. It took Everly a moment to realize he truly wasn't. The man wasn't doing anything that came through as dangerous, and he was wearing what appeared to be a guard's uniform.

Everly didn't shift back right away, instead eyeing the man. His brown hair was cut short, and his brown eyes told Everly he was shocked. He was tall, but not as tall as Everly was in his human form. Everly was fairly sure he could have taken him on even in his human form, although it wouldn't have been pleasant.

Fighting never was.

"Hi," the man said. "Cam said he was expecting a shifter. I'm guessing that's you?"

Everly huffed at his own stupidity. Instead of shifting, he should have asked this man who he was and what he wanted. He was the one invading pack territory, after all. What had he expected? To be allowed to traipse all over the place without anyone asking him who the fuck he was?

He shifted back, looking down at the shreds of fabric that had fallen to the ground. He couldn't afford to lose any more clothes, not until he went shopping, and he wasn't looking forward to it. He didn't like shopping, especially for clothes.

"My name is Everly," he told the man.

The man nodded as if it meant something to him. "Cam mentioned you by name. I'm Kyle."

Kyle was smiling, and Everly found himself smiling back without meaning to. "It's a pleasure to meet you, and I apologize for reacting that way," he said.

Kyle shrugged. "I shouldn't have come from behind. I know rare shifters are kind of touchy."

"Do you?"

Everly found Kyle fascinating, although he didn't quite understand why. He was just a wolf shifter, as far as Everly could tell. Maybe it was because he'd taken all of this in as if it were perfectly normal. He also was trying very hard not to stare at Everly's body and failing miserably. His cheeks were flushed, making him look more adorable than dangerous, and Everly found himself smiling.

"My brother-in-law is a rare shifter. Well, I don't know if I can call him that, since he and Jarvis aren't married or anything like that, but you know what I mean."

"I suppose I do. So you have experience with rare shifters?"

"Not a lot. Peregrine doesn't like me very much, although I hope to change that soon. But I'm sure you want to grab new clothes. Cam and the others have been expecting you, so they're waiting in Cam's house. We can go whenever you're ready."

Right. Everly was here for a reason, and it wasn't to stare at Kyle and imagine what he would like in his bed, unfortunately.

Kyle kept a respectful distance between them even now that Everly had shifted back to his human form, and he stayed away as Everly went back to his truck to grab more clothes. He waited for Everly where he'd been standing, looking away the entire time and making it quite evident that he was.

"Ready," Everly said when he was.

Kyle nodded and started walking, and the only thing Everly could do was go after him.

Kyle wanted to know more about Everly. He had so many questions, including what kind of shifter Everly was. He was clearly a rare shifter, but Kyle hadn't been able to identify what kind.

It had been impressive, though. From what he'd been able to see, Everly was part lion, part eagle. He had enormous wings on his back, but instead of being afraid of them, the claws, and the wicked beak, Kyle couldn't wait to see Everly in that form again.

That wouldn't happen anytime soon. Kyle and the others had their orders, and they were supposed to obey.

Today was his first day, and he hadn't expected it to be so interesting. He wasn't doing much at the moment, mostly training, but Cam had wanted him and the other members on the security team to start patrolling the grounds. Kyle hadn't expected to find anything, even after Cam had told them to keep an eye out for Everly. He was glad he'd been the one to find the man, though.

He kept his distance from Everly, since the other shifter seemed quite jumpy. Kyle didn't know anything about him, but he'd spoken to several rare shifters, and he knew all of them were hunted. That was probably the case with Everly, too, and the last thing Kyle wanted to do was spook him. That was why he stayed away, even though there was nothing he wanted more than to move closer and ask him about a dozen questions.

They reached Cam's house, and Kyle quickly knocked on the door before opening it. Everly arched a brow, maybe at the familiar way Kyle was acting, but the pack was tiny, and the kids had always been welcome in every single house. They'd especially been welcome here, in the alpha's house, and that hadn't changed after the old alpha died and Cam had taken his place.

"Cam?" Kyle called out, even though he knew he'd find the alpha in his office.

Sure enough, that was where Cam appeared a few moments later. He smiled at Kyle, then turned his attention to Everly. "I wasn't sure you'd find the place."

"It wasn't hard. I'm Everly."

Cam nodded. "I'm Camden, the Rosewood pack alpha. Please, call me Cam." He looked at Kyle. "Thank you."

Kyle wanted nothing more than to stay for whatever meeting was about to happen, but it wasn't his place. He'd done his job, and Cam didn't need him here for what was next.

Kyle nodded at him. "It's my job."

"I suppose it is. Why don't you take an hour off work to have lunch with your brother?"

Kyle was pretty sure that wasn't how things usually worked, but the security team was new, and he supposed Cam could do whatever he wanted, considering he was the alpha. "Thank you."

"And let me know if you need help finding your own place or if you want me to talk to your mother."

Kyle grimaced. "I appreciate the offer, but you *really* don't want to talk to her."

Camden barked out a laugh. "I don't. It doesn't mean I won't do it if you need my help."

"For now, I'm fine. But she'll realize I'm not coming back eventually, and I might need you then."

"You know where to find me when that happens. Don't let her walk all over you, Kyle. I'm proud of the man you've become."

That meant a lot to Kyle, since his mother didn't seem to be proud of him.

After one last glance at Everly, Kyle walked away. Since he had time for lunch, he headed home, and by that, he meant Jarvis and Peregrine's home. He'd agreed to stay with them until he could find another place, and while he hadn't gone back to his mother's house to pack his things, he would have to eventually. But today was his first day of work, and he'd wanted to focus on that rather than fighting with his mom.

Jarvis had worked this morning, so Kyle knew he'd find him home when he got there. He smiled when he stepped into the house and smelled food cooking. Hopefully, there would be enough for all of them, although Kyle wouldn't be offended if there wasn't.

"What are you doing here?" Jarvis asked when Kyle walked into the kitchen.

"Cam sent me home for lunch."

Jarvis nodded. "That's good. I cooked pasta, although it's going to need to be in the oven for a bit. How long do you have?"

"About an hour."

"This should be ready in about thirty minutes." He hesitated, and for some reason, Kyle steeled himself. He knew his brother wouldn't hurt him, but it was still his first instinct. "Since we have half an hour, what do you think about going to pack some of your stuff? I realize you won't be able to bring everything from your bedroom to our guest room, but you'll need at least a bag of clothes."

Kyle groaned. "Do I really have to?"

"I mean, you can continue wearing your uniform and the same change of clothes you had when you came here yesterday, but you probably don't want that. Besides, Mom isn't going to let you disappear. She gave you time yesterday, but it's not going to last. She'll expect you tonight, and if you don't go home, she'll come here."

Because Kyle's presence would bring her straight to Jarvis's door, which was the last thing he wanted. Jarvis and their mother weren't talking, and Kyle understood why. He was firmly on Jarvis's side, and that wasn't going to change.

But Jarvis was right. He needed to face their mother, and the sooner he did it, the better it would be.

He sighed. "Fine. I'm going."

"I'm coming with you."

"You don't have to. I know you don't want to talk to her, and I can deal with her on my own."

"But you don't *have* to. That's what brothers are for, isn't it?"

Kyle reacted out instinctively, grabbing Jarvis and pulling him into his arms. Jarvis squeaked, but he hugged Kyle back after only a few moments.

"Thank you," Kyle murmured.

Jarvis patted Kyle's back. "You're welcome. It meant a lot to me that you came here yesterday and apologized, and I want to be here for you."

Kyle wasn't going to argue, even though he felt he didn't deserve it.

Since they only had half an hour before they needed to be home, they headed out right away. Kyle was hoping their mother would be out, but of course, he wasn't that lucky. Her car was parked in front of the house. She seemed to have been waiting for him, because he wasn't even on the porch before the door flew open.

"Finally," Kyle's mother said, staring at him. "Where have you been? Couldn't you have called to tell me you were okay? I was worried."

"Sorry. I didn't mean to worry you, but I needed some time away."

"I hope it was enough for you to realize how stupid your decisions yesterday were. Have you called the college to tell them you changed your mind?"

Kyle sucked in a breath. Not only had their mother ignored what he'd told her yesterday, but she also wasn't looking at Jarvis, who was awkwardly hovering behind Kyle. It was as if he didn't exist, and it made Kyle angry.

"Jarvis is here," he said even though she had to have seen him.

She continued to ignore Jarvis. "And why are you wearing this uniform?" she asked.

At the moment, Kyle hated her. How could she ignore one of her children? How could she ignore what Kyle wanted from his life and what he'd said yesterday? She wanted things always to go her way, but it wasn't always possible, and this situation was a perfect example of that.

He swallowed. Even though he was convinced of what he was doing, it still wasn't easy. "I'm wearing this uniform because today is my first day of work. I just have enough time on my lunch break to pack a few things, since I'm moving into Jarvis's guest room."

That finally got Kyle's mother's attention. "You're doing no such thing."

"I'm sorry, but you don't make my decisions for me. I'm twenty-four, not fourteen. I'm going to pack my things now, and I'm going to leave."

"I won't allow you to do that."

"Haven't you heard what I just said? You don't have to allow anything."

Kyle gently pushed past her and into the house. She moved away, thankfully, and he headed for the stairs, Jarvis right behind him. Jarvis kept peeking at their mother, and Kyle wondered what he thought. Was he afraid of her, or did he want her to react to his presence? Did he miss her? They'd never had a great relationship, and Kyle doubted it would get better unless their mom got her head out of her ass and realized how bad she was behaving.

He started climbing the stairs, Jarvis still behind him.

"I'm warning you," their mom said. "If you leave this house today, this won't be your home anymore."

Kyle had expected that kind of emotional blackmail, so he wasn't surprised. It still hurt, but he could deal with it. "If that's how you feel, I'm sorry, but it doesn't change my mind. I'm moving out, Mom, and that's final, whatever you think about it."

But it looked like Kyle was going to have to talk to Cam sooner than he'd thought he'd have to.

CHAPTER THREE

Everly looked around. The house he'd been offered wasn't empty, thank fuck, but it didn't feel like his. It *wasn't* his, since he'd just arrived the day before, and he'd barely had the time to look around.

After Kyle had deposited him at the alpha's house, Everly, Cam, his beta, and a slew of other people, had a meeting. Arvin had been present on a video conference call. Everly had been honest about why he was on the run. He didn't want anyone to get hurt, especially not these people, who'd welcomed him even when they didn't need to. Cam hadn't seemed worried about the guys after Everly, though. He'd listened to what Everly had to say. Then he'd pointed out that Peregrine had been in pretty much the same position when he'd arrived, yet, he'd managed to find a place with the pack. He hadn't told Everly to do the same, but the way Arvin had looked at Everly, it had been obvious.

And Everly kind of wanted to be able to call this place home.

He'd been surprised when Cam had offered him one of the empty houses that sat on pack territory. There had been more pack members in the past, so many houses were available. Everly hadn't asked why they sat empty. He'd traveled enough and had gotten to know enough people to realize that a lot of shifter groups had seen their numbers dwindle over the past few decades. He'd accepted the offer, and now, here he was.

When he'd stepped into the house after Cam had walked him to it, he'd found everything ready for him. Someone had gone shopping, and the fridge and the cupboards were full in the kitchen. The bathroom had been stocked, too, and there were a few changes of clothes in the bedroom. The sight of all of that had made Everly's eyes prickle, and they still did when he thought about it.

It looked like as soon as Arvin had called him, Cam had worked on making this place a home for Everly, and Everly didn't know how to thank him. He'd wanted to do so yesterday, but as soon as he'd stretched out on the bed after his shower, he'd fallen asleep. He'd slept through the day and part of the night, and when he'd woken up, he'd stayed in bed, feeling safe for the first time in a long time. He knew it wouldn't last, but for now, he had every intention of taking advantage of it. He could relax, stop running, and maybe even imagine he could settle down here.

Everly had gotten out of bed with the sun and had walked around the house. It wasn't huge, but there were three bedrooms, which were two more than he needed. All the necessary furniture was there, but there weren't personal touches, which made sense. If he stayed, he might start buying things to make the house feel like his, but in the meantime, this was more than good enough. He'd have even been happy with a room somewhere, so this was incredible.

But Everly was used to small apartments and being on his own, so he knew that getting used to living with the pack wouldn't be easy. He didn't know anyone but the people who'd been in the meeting yesterday, plus Kyle, the guy who'd first found him. Cam had told him about a small gym he'd put together after he decided to form a security team, though, so Everly decided to head there.

Everly kept himself in shape. It was necessary when people kept hunting him, and it had been useful many times. He didn't like fighting, and he hated blood, but he didn't hesitate to spill it if it meant he could continue living and be free. It wasn't fun to train, but it had saved his life more than once.

The lights were already on when he reached the gym. He hesitated, wondering if he'd interrupt someone, but he supposed he might as well start meeting people. He was sure everyone knew about his presence by now. That was how small packs usually worked. Once one person knew something, the news spread like wildfire. He was surprised no one had knocked on his door yet, although someone still might.

He carefully pushed open the door and peeked inside. Someone had turned on some music. Several people were already working out, which surprised Everly since it was so early. A woman was running on a treadmill, earbuds in her ears. A man was sitting on a bench, drying his sweaty face with a towel. There were other people, but once Everly noticed Kyle in a corner, he was the only one he could see.

Kyle hadn't seen Everly, or at least, Everly didn't think so. He was talking with someone with a bright smile on his face. The other man clasped Kyle's shoulder, and Kyle moved toward one of the empty treadmills.

"Good morning," a voice said behind Everly.

Everly hadn't even heard Cam, which was a surprise. He was usually more careful than this, but he supposed that he felt safe enough not to be. That was surprising, too. He'd just gotten to Rosewood, so it shouldn't feel like home already.

Everly forced a smile. "Good morning."

"Are you here to train?"

"That was the idea, yes."

"You can go in. I wouldn't have told you about the gym if you weren't welcome to use it."

"I don't want to bother anyone."

"You won't. The team is training, but they're just starting."

Cam had told Everly yesterday about the security team he'd put together, and Everly was curious. He was surprised Cam hadn't created the team sooner, although he supposed the pack hadn't needed it. Now that several rare shifters lived here, they and the rest of the pack needed to be protected.

Everly had never had anyone to protect him. Even when he'd been a teenager, he'd been in foster care. No one had cared what happened to him, and sometimes he wondered if anyone had even noticed he'd run away. The pack was like a family, though. Everly didn't need to meet more people to be aware of that. Seeing how the people who'd been at the meeting yesterday behaved with each other had been enough.

"Let's go in," Cam said. "We'll get coffee once we're done, and we can talk more if you want. Or you can go home and rest. I'm sure that after being on the run for so long, you could do with an entire day in bed."

"I wouldn't mind having the possibility of doing just that, but I think it would feel strange."

Everly followed Cam inside. A few people noticed them this time, and the guy Kyle had been talking to grinned and walked closer. Kyle didn't see them, but he was running on the treadmill, looking the other way.

"Hey, Cam," the man said once he reached them.

Cam seemed familiar with him. Everly had been surprised at how everyone acted as if Cam was their big brother rather than the alpha, but he'd already realized that was how Cam was. He didn't want people to bow down to him or treat him like he was their king. He was the alpha, yes, but that didn't mean he had absolute control. He kept the pack safe and needed its members to obey when it came to that, but as far as Everly had been able to see, he didn't stick his nose into the members' lives unless he absolutely had to.

"Bryson, this is Everly," Cam said. "He arrived yesterday."

Bryson nodded and offered Everly his hand. "The guy you told me about?"

"Yes, Arvin's friend. Everly, this is Bryson, my brother."

Everly shook Bryson's hand. "It's a pleasure to meet you."

"Same. We're happy to have you with us," Bryson said.

Everly was starting to realize that was the truth, even though he had a hard time understanding why. But everyone he'd talked to so far seemed to be happy to have him here, even though they knew how much trouble he could bring. It didn't seem to matter, not beyond telling him that the pack would fight beside him if something happened. It wasn't something Everly was used to, and he didn't quite know how to deal with it.

He supposed that making friends was one way to make that happen, and he hoped he wasn't too rusty. It had been a long time since he'd made a friend.

Once Kyle had seen Everly from the corner of his eye, he couldn't focus on what he was doing anymore. He kept peeking at Everly, Bryson, and Cam, wondering what they were telling each other. The conversation seemed to be going well, and Everly was smiling, making him look more relaxed. Kyle had noticed how gorgeous Everly was yesterday, but he thought Everly was even more beautiful now, after what had to have been a good night's sleep.

Kyle desperately wanted to know Everly's story. He wanted to ask why Everly was here and whether the stories he'd heard around the pack were true. Everly seemed to be a rare shifter, from what Kyle had seen yesterday, but he still wasn't sure what kind. The easiest way to find out would be to ask, but Everly was talking with Cam and Bryson, and Kyle didn't want to interrupt them or look like an idiot, which sometimes happened when he was with people he liked.

Everly wasn't the kind of guy Kyle usually went for. Kyle liked people who were smaller than him, male or female. He wasn't into the muscle look, preferring slender people who didn't look like they could bench press him.

But Everly was taller than Kyle, who was tall to begin with. His shoulders were wide, and his arms bulging with muscles. His long blond hair was bound at his nape, and he was wearing a pair of shorts and a t-shirt. He looked like he belonged here in the gym.

Kyle was so busy staring at Everly that it took him a moment to realize Cam was waving at him to come closer. When he did, he almost fell on his face as he misplaced a foot on the treadmill. Thankfully, he managed to grab the handles and didn't make a fool of himself. He was pretty sure no one had noticed what he'd just done, at least until he reached the little group. Once there, he noticed how Everly's eyes glittered, and he knew the other man had seen him.

Kyle sighed. Trust him to look like an idiot in front of a guy he found attractive.

He plastered a smile on his face. It wouldn't help to dwell on what had just happened, and besides, Everly didn't seem offended. If anything, he looked amused, which was better than having him make fun of Kyle.

"You needed me?" he asked Cam.

"Bryson and I were talking to Everly, and he mentioned something about his house being too big for him," Cam said. "He agrees that having a roommate would probably be for the best, and I know you need a place to stay."

Kyle blinked. That wasn't what he'd expected when Cam had waved him over, but it wasn't bad news. He'd only moved in with his brother and Peregrine yesterday, and while he loved them, he also wasn't sure he could stay in the long run. They were sweet and had made him feel welcome, but it was obvious he was encroaching on their private space and they weren't used to having to share it. He'd walked in on them making out on the table in the kitchen this morning, and he was pretty sure that if he'd been even ten minutes later, they'd have been half-naked.

He loved his brother, but he did *not* want to see him naked.

Kyle eyed Everly. "And you think *I* should be his roommate?"

"I don't see why not. You need a place, and Everly has the space. Besides, Everly is new here, and I'm sure he could use some company."

Kyle wanted to be that company, but he wondered if it was a good idea. He found Everly gorgeous, even though he wasn't usually his type. He was also so interesting that Kyle wanted to ask him question after question about him and his life. That could become irritating fast, even if Kyle managed to keep his mouth under control for a bit.

On the other hand, he'd catch Peregrine and Jarvis naked if he didn't move out soon, so as long as he acted normal, he shouldn't have a problem living with Everly.

"As long as it's fine with Everly, I don't have a problem with it," Kyle said.

"It's fine with me," Everly confirmed. He was still smiling, and now it felt like the smile was just for Kyle.

That was going to become a problem if Kyle wasn't careful, but he didn't have to think about it yet. He was eager to get to know Everly and happy to have already found his own place. He'd have a roommate, but frankly, he was happy about that, too. He'd thought about getting his own apartment, but he'd never lived alone, and he'd wondered if he'd get lonely. Now, he wouldn't have to find out.

"Right," Cam said, a big smile on his face. "I'm sure the two of you can find a way to make it work. Kyle, let me know if you need help moving your stuff from your parents' house. I know your mother isn't going to take this well."

Kyle grimaced. "She already hasn't. Jarvis and I went over yesterday to get some clothes, since I'm staying in his guest room at the moment."

"Well, if you need my help, you know where to find me."

Kyle nodded and turned back to Everly. "I'm sure you want to train now, and I have to get back to it, too. We can talk later?"

Everly nodded. "We'll talk after the gym."

There was a bounce in Kyle's step as he went back to the treadmill. He couldn't believe what had just happened. He'd been worried about having to stay with Jarvis and Peregrine for too long and curious about Everly. Now, it seemed both those things would be resolved by him moving in with Everly, and he couldn't wait. He just had to make sure not to make a fool of himself.

Easier said than done, but Kyle supposed that if he and Everly lived together, Everly would realize how much of an idiot Kyle was eventually.

Kyle hopped back onto the treadmill and started running. He was distracted, but that wasn't surprising. He kept peeking in Everly's direction as Everly started training with Cam and Bryson. Everly and Bryson seemed to be friends already, and Kyle wondered if that was the kind of guy Everly was attracted to. Kyle and Bryson couldn't be more different, so maybe Kyle wouldn't have a chance with Everly.

"You're going to fall on your face," someone said from beside Kyle.

Kyle startled hard enough to miss a step. He stumbled, then straightened and glared at his best friend. "What are you doing here?"

Marcus grinned. "I thought it was obvious. I'm running."

He was on the treadmill beside Kyle's. "It's seven in the morning. Why aren't you asleep in your bed? Or getting ready to go to class?"

Marcus bit his lower lip and looked away, a sure sign he was hiding something from Kyle. Kyle waited, knowing that pushing wouldn't help. When Marcus had a secret, the only way Kyle found out about it was by waiting and giving him the time that he needed to say what he had on his mind.

Kyle focused on the sound of his footsteps until Marcus finally said, "I signed up for the team."

The surprise was enough to make Kyle almost fall again, at which point he decided the treadmill wasn't for him today. He turned it off, then hopped to the floor and grabbed his towel. "What does that mean?" he asked as he dried his face.

Marcus followed Kyle's lead and turned his treadmill off, too. "Exactly what I said. I signed up for the team."

"What about college?"

"I didn't quit, if that's what you're asking. But when I heard about this team, I realized what I wanted to do with my life."

"Be a security guard?" It was enough for Kyle, but it never would be for Marcus. He was too bright, and if he gave himself the opportunity, he'd do great things.

"To begin with. But I want to help with the computer side of the security system, too, and when I told Cam about it, he agreed. Eventually, once I finish college, I'll be in charge of it, or at least, that's what I hope for. I thought it would be a good idea to be part of the security team, too, to see how things worked and get the lay of the land."

Kyle cocked his head. "You already know the lay of the land. You were born here."

Marcus punched Kyle's shoulder. "You know what I mean. Anyway, I'm here, and I'm here to stay. We don't need to talk about it."

But Kyle wanted to. If this was what Marcus wanted to do, Kyle was all for it, though.

"Tell me about the gorgeous blond training with Bryson," Marcus said.

Kyle felt the need to growl at him, but he clamped his mouth shut. Everly wasn't his, and if Marcus wanted to ask him out, there was nothing Kyle could do about it. "That's

Everly, the new guy."

Marcus slowly nodded. "I see. Everyone's talking about him, and I understand why now."

Kyle sighed. "He's gorgeous, isn't he?"

"He is, but he's nothing like the kind of guys you usually date."

"I know."

Marcus bumped their shoulders together. "That doesn't mean it's a bad thing. I could see the two of you together."

Kyle wasn't sure that was the case, but he supposed he'd find out soon.

"Arvin mentioned something about the pack needing help with the security system," Everly said.

It had been a while since he'd trained with anyone, but he found that Cam could keep up with him. Everly might not like doing this, but it was a necessity, and he wouldn't let anyone hold him back. That certainly wasn't the case here, with everyone training.

Cam was on one side of Everly, with Bryson on the other. Bryson was mostly silent, allowing Cam and Everly to have their conversation. Everly hadn't been sure what to ask, but he wanted these people to become his friends. It would be hell when he had to move on and leave them behind, but he'd had enough of being alone. No matter how much he enjoyed his own company, he wanted and deserved friends.

"He told me you were into computers," Cam said.

"I am. I created the rare shifters network."

Cam nodded as if he knew what it was. He probably did, since he knew Arvin and Peregrine. "You saved Peregrine's life."

"Us rare shifters have to stick together."

"There's safety in numbers."

"Actually, for us, there usually isn't. That's why I was so surprised when I realized you were welcoming so many rare shifters. Aren't you afraid of the trouble that follows us?"

Cam took a moment to answer, which Everly liked.

"That fear is always there, of course," Cam finally said. "And we've had a fair share of trouble since Toby and Sam stumbled into our lives. It was easier when Sage was the only rare shifter with us, but I can't say I'm sorry we found everyone else. I found my mate, for one, and so did other pack members. That alone is enough for me to want to welcome other rare shifters, but it's also the fact that you shouldn't have to run your entire life. You deserve a place to call home if that's what you want."

And Everly wanted it. He wasn't sure it was doable, but he had the feeling that if it was, Cam would be the person to make it happen.

"But going back to the security system, I'd like it if you could go over what we already have and make any changes you think are necessary," Cam continued. "We've never had to implement these measures before."

"Because with so many rare shifters, the people hunting them aren't far behind."

Cam's expression was grim as he nodded. "Exactly. We were lucky enough when we got Toby back that the gang who had him didn't try to hunt him down, but others weren't so lucky. Peregrine especially had to deal with those people finding him, and I don't want him to feel like he has to go on the run ever again."

"I'll be happy to go over everything and see what I can do to make it better," Everly said, meaning every word.

He'd never had much hope of finding a place to call home, and he still didn't, but he felt like maybe this time, he at least had a chance. He didn't know what would come out of it or if anything would at all, but if this was his only possibility to have a home, he'd make sure to take it. That meant making the pack as safe as possible, both for himself and the other rare shifters who lived here.

And it was a new challenge. Everly spent most of his time working on the rare shifters network, plus doing some other work on the side to earn money. Thankfully, working on his computer made it easy for him to move every time he had to. He'd never had to implement a security system for an entire pack, usually limiting himself to his apartment. It should be fun, and he couldn't wait to start.

He was surprised to realize that he trusted Cam, even though they'd only met yesterday. The alpha seemed to be a good person, and of course, Everly had done his research before he'd gotten here. There was nothing that said that Cam would betray him, which made it even easier to accept doing this.

"Unfortunately, we don't have much at the moment," Cam continued. "We've had a lot to deal with recently, and I only decided to put together a security team and the security system a few weeks ago."

"I think it's impressive, especially for a pack that never had to deal with any of this before."

Cam nodded. His muscles bulged as he raised his weights. "It's always only been wolves, at least until Sage. Even when there were more members, my father never had to worry about fencing in pack territory and keeping an eye on people who sniffed around. We have a lot fewer members than when my father was in his prime, which is why we were able to find you a house so easily. It's been empty for a while."

"I noticed that, and I was curious. I know shifters, in general, have diminishing numbers, but it seems extreme here."

"It was, for a while. At the end of my father's life, we didn't even reach fifty members. I'm sure you can imagine how it is, with elderly shifters dying, young ones moving away from a small town, taking their children with them. Then we started having an influx of new shifters. I'm more than happy to welcome them here, and not just because more members means the pack is stronger. I kind of like the idea of being a safe haven for rare shifters, especially since there aren't many of those."

"I can confirm that." Everly had been moving around the country for half his life. He could count the fingers of one hand how many packs and shifter groups had welcomed rare shifters without trying to manipulate or use them.

The thought of helping Cam put this together excited him. He'd done what he could with the network, warning the rare shifters when someone was after them and helping them find a new place to live, but it never felt like enough. It had been the only thing he could afford to do at the time, but now, with Cam and the Rosewood pack by his side, he could move forward. He'd have to talk to Cam about it, but it would be better to wait for a bit until he was settled. Cam had to focus on his existing pack before thinking about helping more people.

"We've been working with other packs," Cam said, still focused on his weights. "The Springfield pack nearby is a bust because of how they treated Owen and Toby, but there are others, some of them quite big. Unfortunately, after my father died, I lost contact with some of the alphas. I really shouldn't have, but I was grieving, and I had to deal with this pack. Now, I'm trying to work with them, and it's not always easy."

"You're putting together a real-life network."

Cam grinned. "That's what I'm trying to do, yes. I want to find alphas who, like me, believe that rare shifters should be treated like any shifter. I'd like to find other alphas willing to open their pack and make them a safe haven for rare shifters."

"And have you?" Because this would be easier if the Rosewood pack had allies.

Cam nodded. "We're still in the earlier stages, but I

contacted the Wakefield pack. They're bigger than us, and they've agreed to help if we need it. Our relationship is new, but I'm hoping it'll change in time."

"I'm sure it will."

Maybe Everly could put together another network for the alphas willing to help rare shifters. He could put rare shifters on the run in contact with the alphas whose pack was safe for them, and it would make life easier for a lot of people.

Having all these ideas was exciting, and Everly couldn't wait to start, even though he wasn't quite sure where to begin. With so many ideas and things to do, it wouldn't be easy to prioritize. Thankfully, for once, it looked like he wouldn't be working on his own. He'd always had to, which meant he'd been responsible for every aspect of every project, plus keeping himself safe.

For now, he didn't have to worry about that. He was surrounded by shifters who would step in if someone tried to hurt him. That meant he could focus on putting together the security system Cam needed and making pack territory as safe as possible. Once that was done, he'd move on to putting together the network between alphas and putting out the word that Rosewood was safe.

For once, he had a chance at really making a difference, and he wouldn't waste it.

Kyle wished Everly had given him time to take a shower before talking to him after the gym. He'd waved at Kyle as soon as Kyle was done, and Kyle couldn't do anything but go to him.

"You're ready to talk?" he asked when he reached Everly.

Everly had put away everything he'd used during his session, and he nodded. He looked distracted, though, and he kept peeking around. "You smell that?" he asked.

Kyle's cheeks flushed. "Sorry, I'm pretty sure that's me. I haven't showered yet."

Everly's eyes widened, and he looked like he was about to laugh. "I didn't mean it in a bad way. There's something here that smells heavenly."

Kyle sniffed. He hadn't noticed it before, but under the stink of sweaty guys and mats, he could smell something enthralling. "That's strange," he said.

Everly shrugged. "Anyway, I wanted to talk about you moving in with me."

Kyle nodded eagerly and made sure to keep his distance from Everly. The man might not be offended that he stank, but he didn't want to risk it. "I've been thinking about getting my own place for a while now. I just had a fight with my mother, and I'm staying with my brother for now, but he met his mate recently, and I'm terrified I'm going to walk in on them in a state I don't want to see."

This time, Everly did laugh. "I can imagine. Well, I don't have a problem with it. The house Cam gave me is much too big for me. There are three bedrooms, and while one of them is small, the other is just a bit smaller than the master bedroom I chose. You could have that one, or I could move out of the master bedroom if you'd rather have it."

It was tempting to say yes just to have the opportunity to sleep in a bed Everly had slept in, but Kyle shook his head. He was starting to creep himself out with how attracted he was to Everly and how nuts he and his wolf were about the guy. "The bigger guest room will be fine. When can I move in?"

"Whenever you want. I've never had a roommate, though, so I'm not sure what we should do. Would it be worth it to put together a set of rules?"

"The only people I've ever lived with are my parents and my siblings, so I'm not sure where to start, either. I suppose as long as we respect each other's spaces, everything will be good, and we can put rules together as we go? Unless you have something more specific in mind."

"Not for now, but I can think about it. You should, too, as you pack your things."

"There's not much to pack, so I should be ready to move in about an hour."

"I'll be at home waiting for you."

Everly explained which house Cam had given him, making sure Kyle would be able to find it. Kyle remembered the lady who'd lived there. She'd passed away several years ago, and neither of her kids had come back. Her house had sat empty since then, and he was happy someone would be living in it again.

He rushed home after saying goodbye to Everly, eager for a shower and getting back to the man. He didn't stop to chat with his brother, who he could hear in the kitchen. First, he needed to get clean.

As soon as he was out of the shower, he threw on the first jeans and t-shirt he found, pushed everything else into his bags, and dragged them down the stairs. He dropped them by the front door, then finally went to find his brother.

Kyle was happy he wouldn't have to stay with Jarvis and Peregrine for too long, but he was also sorry to be moving out so soon. He'd enjoyed spending time with his brother, and he had to remind himself that he wasn't losing Jarvis. They might not share the same house anymore, but it didn't mean they couldn't see each other as often as they wanted to.

"I thought I'd heard you," Jarvis said. He was sitting at the table, already dressed for work. He had a later shift today, which explained why he was still here.

Kyle flopped into one of the other chairs at the table. "I went to the gym. Cam was there, as well as the new guy, Everly."

Jarvis bounced a little in his chair. "Peregrine told me about him. He saved Peregrine's life, and I can't wait to meet him."

"Well, he's going to be my new roommate, so you'll have plenty of opportunities to do just that."

Jarvis's eyes widened. "You're going to live with him?"

"Cam put it together. The house he gave Everly is too big, so Cam asked if I wanted to move in with him. Everly was okay with it, and I said yes. As much as I love living with you, I know you and Peregrine want your privacy back."

Jarvis's cheeks went red. "Maybe, but I liked having you around, even though it was only for a few days."

"Me moving out doesn't mean we won't see each other anymore. Now that I have you back, I'm not letting you go."

Jarvis beamed. "Good, because I feel the same. You need help moving your stuff?"

"It's only a few bags, so I'll be okay. Besides, I'm sure that now that you have an empty house, Peregrine will want to drag you back into bed."

Jarvis's cheeks were so red that he looked like he was about to spontaneously combust. "I have to go to work."

Kyle laughed. "I was just teasing. I'm glad we had these few days, though, and I'm happy you found Peregrine. You were never happy when we still lived at home, but now you are, and I'm so glad."

"And I'm glad to have you back in my life. I never thought we could have this kind of relationship, and I'm not going to allow anyone to put distance between us again."

Jarvis was a bit teary by the time Kyle was ready to go and he needed to go to work. They hugged a few times, then Jarvis headed for his car while Kyle grabbed his bags and started the short walk to what was now his home.

Even after the owner had passed away, the pack had kept it in shape, so it looked good, if a bit anonymous. There were no flowers in the small yard in front of it and no personal objects on the porch. Kyle didn't know how long he'd live with Everly, but he couldn't wait to make the place truly his.

He climbed the porch steps and knocked. It only took Everly a few moments to open, and when he did, he grinned. "I never thought to ask where your brother lives."

Kyle turned around and pointed at Jarvis's house. "See that house? It's that one. The house I grew up in is just a bit further away. Everyone lives close by in the pack."

"I guess I'm going to have to get used to that."

"Just like you're going to have to get used to the fact that everyone knows your business. It's like living in a small town."

"Well, Rosewood is small."

Kyle snickered. "Then we're a small town in a small town. I hope you're not planning on having any secrets, because you won't be able to keep them for any length of time."

Everly stepped to the side to let Kyle in.

Kyle walked into the house, but his attention was on Everly. Everly's hair was still damp from the shower, and his t-shirt was sticking a bit to his skin. He was wearing jeans, but his feet were bare. He looked more relaxed, and Kyle hoped it meant he was thinking of staying and eventually making Rosewood his home.

"I can smell that scent again," Everly grumbled.

"I promise I showered." Everly laughed, which was what Kyle had been aiming for. He dropped his bags at the foot of the stairs and looked around. "This looks good."

"It does. It's a bit impersonal for now, but it won't be for long. You want me to show you around?"

"You don't need to. Growing up, every kid went into every house. We're like a big family. But I haven't seen the house recently, so I guess you could."

Everly stepped closer. "Or maybe we could do something different."

Kyle was pretty sure his heart was about to beat out of his chest like in one of those corny cartoons. He licked his lips, wondering what was going on. "I don't know. What did you have in mind?"

Everly stepped even closer, and Kyle took a deep breath. That was when he realized what the scent Everly had smelled was. He opened his mouth to tell Everly, although he had no idea what to say, but before a word could cross his lips, Everly was on him.

He wrapped his arms around Kyle's back and pulled him close. Kyle went, his mind still reeling at the thought that Everly was his mate. That didn't make him push Everly away, though, and when Everly kissed him, he kissed back. He buried his hands into Everly's long hair, gently pulling and using it to angle Everly's mouth to give him better access. Everly's scent filled his nose, and he wanted so much more.

Thankfully, after a while, he got back into himself. He wanted to continue kissing Everly, but first, they had to talk. "I figured out what that smell is," he murmured.

Everly's lips were so close that Kyle would only have to lean forward just a bit to kiss him again. He looked dazed. "What do you mean?"

"It's twice now that you mentioned a scent you noticed. I know what it is."

"Yeah?"

Kyle took a deep breath. "It's me. You smell delicious to me, too, and there's a good reason for that."

"We showered."

Kyle laughed. "We did, but that's not what I'm talking about. What you smell is me, and the reason I smell like that is that we're mates."

CHAPTER FOUR

W*e're mates*. Everly couldn't stop thinking about those words, even though Kyle had said them a few days ago.

He stared at his computer screen, but he wasn't seeing it. All his thoughts were on Kyle and what was happening between them. He hadn't expected to find his mate when he moved in with the Rosewood pack. He'd never given much thought to having a mate, convinced that if he ever found his mate, he'd have to leave them behind. He still wasn't sure that he wouldn't, which was one of the reasons he was so hesitant.

He and Kyle hadn't talked about it. They should, but Everly had obviously freaked out after Kyle told him and Everly realized it was true, and Kyle had said they could wait. It was obvious he desperately wanted to talk about it every time they were together, and they would, but not yet.

Everything in Everly's life was a mess. He'd had to leave his apartment, and he was in a new place, surrounded by new people. He was making friends, but he still hadn't found his footing, and he wasn't sure what to do about Kyle. It would be nice to have a boyfriend, but was Everly ready for a *mate*? More importantly, was Kyle prepared for a mate like Everly?

Everly wouldn't find out if he didn't talk to Kyle, but it had been easier to make out with him every evening after work. That way, they didn't *have* to talk, and Everly could pretend everything was all right. He wouldn't be able to do that much longer, but at the moment, it was a lifeline he wasn't ready to give up.

He didn't even know what he wanted. To continue making

out with Kyle, of course, but what came next? Could Everly and Kyle be together in the long term? Everly didn't even know if he'd be able to stay in Rosewood. He was starting to want to more than he'd ever wanted to stay anywhere, and he knew the people here wanted him to stay, too, but was it possible? What if he and Kyle got together, and Everly had to run? He couldn't do that to Kyle or himself, but he wasn't sure Kyle would understand.

All in all, Everly had no idea what he and Kyle were doing, what they'd do in the future, or what it meant for them to be mates. He knew what he wanted, which was to stay, but not how to make it happen. He was still convinced he couldn't bring his problems to Rosewood, and he wasn't going to change his mind. The pack had welcomed him with open arms, and he'd feel horrible if they got in trouble because of him. On the other hand, he never wanted to leave, especially now that he had Kyle.

He groaned and raked his hands through his hair. What was he going to do?

He doubted he'd find a solution by daydreaming about Kyle and wondering. He'd never been one to sit back and wait for things to happen, which meant that if he wanted to stay in Rosewood and be with Kyle, he'd have to work for it. He'd always believed it wasn't possible, but was it? Especially now that he wasn't alone anymore, there might be a chance for him to finally be able to settle down and have the life he'd always wanted but had never allowed himself to hope for.

He turned his attention back to his computer screen. If he wanted to stay, he'd have to make Rosewood and pack territory safe for everyone, including him and every other rare shifter. He had no doubt that more would arrive eventually. Everyone wanted a safe place to live their lives, and Rosewood was precisely that. That was also Cam's goal, and it was nice to be working toward that.

And how would Everly make Rosewood safe? It didn't feel possible to protect so many people, and he knew there could still be accidents and trouble, but Cam was fencing pack territory, and once he finished, Everly would be in charge of the security system. He'd already told Cam he was planning on putting cameras everywhere, and while it would somehow restrict the freedom of the pack members, he hoped no one would care. Yes, they'd be filmed if they walked around the fences, and they wouldn't be able to run around the forest as freely as they had before, but this wasn't the goal. The goal was making sure no one snuck in and tried to hurt pack members, and Everly hoped everyone would realize it.

Unfortunately, he was pretty sure that wouldn't be the case.

Most people had been friendly when he'd first met them, but not everyone. He'd especially noticed a woman who kept glaring at him, and he'd been tempted to ask someone what her problem with him was. He didn't really care, though, so he hadn't. If she needed to tell him something, she knew where to find him. Everyone did, which still made Everly feel as if he might be attacked at any moment, even though he knew he wouldn't be. Everyone might know where he lived, but the pack was a family, glaring woman notwithstanding.

Everly's computer beeped, and he looked at what was happening. He grinned when he realized Arvin was calling him and quickly brought up the app on his screen.

"Hello," he said.

Arvin was in his office, relaxed in his seat. He grinned back at Everly. "You look good, better than the last time we had a video call."

"You mean that sleeping full nights and eating regularly is doing wonders for my complexion? I'd never have thought."

Arvin laughed. "You're definitely doing better if you can joke about it. But really, how are you feeling?"

"Better than I have in a long time."

"That's good. I was sure you'd feel better once you were with the pack. You needed someone to make you feel protected, and Cam does."

"I'm still not sure why they're doing it, but at the moment, I don't really care. It just feels good not to have to look over my shoulder every single second of every day." And it was incredible to be able to step out of the house without having to wonder if he'd be able to come back or if someone would capture him.

"They're doing it because it's the right thing to do. I thought you'd have realized that by now."

Everly settled back in his chair. "I have. Everyone has been so nice, and I'm enjoying my time here. It's just hard to believe that this truly could be a safe haven for rare shifters, and especially for me."

"Because you never allowed yourself to think you'd find this."

"I couldn't, because it would have broken me every time I ran. I suppose I'm afraid to hope in this case, too. What if I do, and I end up having to leave?"

Arvin frowned. "Why would you have to run?"

"Some people could find and try to take me."

"Then you stay in pack territory."

"They could find out about this pack and try to grab me here. Hell, they could try to grab any rare shifter. They'd make millions on the black market, and they wouldn't hesitate to kill the Rosewood pack to get to us."

And that thought was terrifying. Most of the people after rare shifters tried to capture them without attracting attention, which meant they didn't kill people. There was nothing worse than drawing attention because you killed someone.

But not everyone was like that. Some people were rich and had a lot of power, and nothing would happen to them even if they killed an entire pack. They'd have someone else deal with it, and that was what scared Everly.

But he and Cam and everyone else here were working on it. Cam had already bought the fence that would go around pack territory, and a team was set to start working on the foundations tomorrow. They'd be human, which meant everyone in the pack would have to be careful not to shift in front of them, but Everly suspected that at least part of the people in town knew something was up and wouldn't be surprised to find out about shifters.

As for Everly, he was working hard on the security system. As soon as the fence was up, he'd be out there to place cameras and alarms. He still didn't know if he was going to stay, but if he was, he'd be safe, along with the rest of the pack.

"Talk me through everything you're doing to keep the pack safe," Arvin said.

Everly grinned. Arvin truly knew him better than he'd realized, but he found he didn't care. If anything, he liked it because it made him feel like he mattered.

And he was starting to realize he did.

Kyle stepped over the branch, glad he'd seen it before his foot could hook under it and he'd fall on his face. Only he, Marcus, and Bryson were around, but that didn't mean he wanted to make a fool of himself. It was happening way too often recently. He'd almost fallen on his face several times at the gym, and now he was afraid of looking like an idiot every time he was with Everly, even after realizing they were mates.

Kyle licked his lips. He looked around, but the only things he could see were trees, trees, and more trees. There was no one here trying to sneak in, which was a relief. Kyle was trying to be a good guard, but he wasn't there yet. No matter how hard he trained and studied, it would take him a while to truly become good at this job.

Everly didn't need Kyle to keep him safe. Unlike most of the people Kyle had dated, he was more than able to keep himself safe. Kyle had no doubt that if they physically fought, Everly would win. He was also smarter than Kyle, something that made Kyle proud but also worried him.

He liked protecting people. He supposed it was one of the reasons he'd become part of the security team. He wanted to protect the pack and his home and for everyone who lived here to be safe. But Everly didn't need protecting. Everly didn't need *Kyle*, and Kyle wasn't sure what to do about it. Was there even anything he could or should do?

"I don't know what's going on in his head," someone said.

Kyle ignored it. It was either Bryson or Marcus, and if they had questions, they'd ask them. Neither was shy about it.

Everly hadn't reacted the way Kyle had expected when he'd told him they were mates. When those words had crossed Kyle's lips, Everly's eyes had widened, and he'd stumbled back. Kyle thought it was a shock. Everly had looked like he had no idea what to do or think, and Kyle felt pretty much the same way. He'd believed they'd talk about it, but instead, after the first moment of surprise, Everly had grabbed him and kissed him again.

That was what happened every evening. Kyle went home after work and showered. He and Everly had dinner. Once that was done, they sat on the couch to watch a movie. They usually ended up making out for most of the movie, and when the movie was over, they headed to their own beds.

Wash and repeat every day.

Kyle hoped things would change over the weekend. He was off patrol duty on Sunday, and he couldn't wait to spend the day with Everly. Was that something Everly would want? Kyle could only hope so, but maybe he should corner Everly and ask him what the fuck they were doing. He wanted to, but he also didn't want to spook Everly, which he suspected would happen if he pushed too much. But what was he supposed to do? Ignore the fact that they were mates? Ignore the fact that they lived together, made out every night, and that Kyle wanted to spend the rest of his life doing it?

Something knocked against his shoulder. He jumped to the side, placing his body into a defensive position before he realized it was Bryson who had touched him. Bryson looked startled for a second, then he grinned. "What were you thinking about that you didn't even hear me call you?"

Kyle hadn't, which was a problem. He was a security guard, and he was on the job. He was supposed to hear everything that happened around him and act accordingly. What if Bryson had been an enemy? What if he'd been here to attack the pack, and Kyle hadn't heard him?

Bryson's smile faded, and he reached for Kyle. "I was teasing. What's going on?"

Kyle shook his head. He didn't know if Everly would want anyone to know about them, not even Kyle's best friends.

Kyle wasn't sure when Bryson had become one of his best friends, but he had. Cam usually assigned the three of them to patrol duty together, and it felt like they'd done this their entire lives. Even Marcus looked like he belonged, even though he'd had to shift a lot of things around to be able to continue going to college while working.

They were a team, and Kyle desperately wanted to tell someone what was going on. He couldn't, but maybe he could tell them part of it.

He looked around, but everything was quiet except for them. When he turned his attention back to Marcus and Bryson, they were both staring. Kyle had no doubt they were worried, and he didn't want them to be. "Sorry. I was thinking."

"That was kind of obvious," Marcus said. "But what were

you thinking about? It's not like you to be so distracted on the job."

"I'll do better," Kyle promised.

Marcus shook his head. "That's not why I said it. I just meant that whatever is on your mind has to be important, considering how much you care about this job. Do you want to talk about it?"

Kyle hesitated. He couldn't tell them he and Everly were mates, but he could mention his feelings for Everly. "It's Everly," he eventually said.

Marcus grinned. "Have you moved into his bed yet?"

Kyle sputtered and didn't see the next root as he started walking away. He stumbled but managed to catch himself against a tree, glared at Marcus, who was clearly trying not to laugh, and straightened. "I haven't moved anywhere," he said.

"But you want to. That's what you were going to tell us, isn't it? You like Everly more than as a roommate."

Kyle sighed. "I do. And we've been making out every day since I moved in with him."

Marcus gaped, but Bryson nodded as if he'd already known. "Everly did say he liked you," he said.

Right. Bryson and Everly had grown close, so it made sense for Everly to talk to Bryson. Kyle was tempted to ask Bryson to tell him everything, but it would feel like a breach of Everly's privacy. It wouldn't be fair, no matter how much Kyle wanted to know. He was glad Everly was finding friends in the pack, and he wanted that to continue.

"I just don't know if there's anything I should do about it," he confessed.

"What do you mean?" Bryson asked.

"I don't know if Everly and I can be together." And it wasn't just because Everly was avoiding talking about the fact that they were mates. "For one, Everly isn't planning to stay, is he? From what I know, he's been on the run his entire adult life, and he doesn't think that's going to change. He's helping us secure pack territory, but I don't know if that'll be enough for him to stay."

And that was one more reason Kyle hadn't pushed to talk about what they were to each other. What if Everly told him it didn't change anything? What if he said he was leaving anyway, no matter how Kyle felt about it?

"You seem to be doing well together," Marcus said, but he sounded more hesitant.

"We're friends." Probably more, considering they kissed every day, but maybe not? It depended on what idea Everly had of friendship. Kyle would never kiss someone who was only a friend, but maybe that wasn't the case for Everly. Maybe he just liked Kyle and wanted someone to kiss.

But they were mates. That had to mean something.

"Maybe you should get him to change his mind about leaving," Bryson said. "I don't think he really wants to, just that he feels he has to. You're right when you say he's been on the run his entire adult life, but I'm pretty sure he doesn't actually want to be. If we want him to stay, we'll have to show him that Rosewood is safe and how much he stands to lose if he runs."

Kyle agreed, but would he be enough? Would his presence here and what he and Everly were to each other be enough to convince Everly to give them a chance and to stay in Rosewood?

Kyle was afraid to find out the answer to those questions.

Everly was excited. His talk with Arvin had helped soothe his worries, and while he still wasn't sure he should stay, he could see himself doing it. He could see himself settling down with Kyle, something he could never have imagined even a week ago. Now, here he was, having found a home and a mate. He and Kyle needed to talk, but first, Everly had to take care of his work.

He'd already put together the bare bones of the network that would allow alphas who wanted to protect rare shifters to contact each other. It wasn't hard, not the communication part anyway. It was harder to keep it safe so no one could hack into the website and find out where the rare shifters were, but Everly had been doing this for years. He knew he could make the website safe, which meant he could keep many shifters and packs safe, including the Rosewood pack.

He was working on the network at the same time as he worked on the pack's security system. He'd already showed Cam where he wanted the cameras, and while he'd been worried there would be too many of them for Cam's taste, Cam hadn't protested. He was ready to do anything to keep the pack safe, and he recognized that the expert in this case was Everly.

It was strange to think of himself as an expert on anything except running. With every hour that passed, though, Everly could see himself settling down in Rosewood more and more, and he wanted to make that dream a reality. He didn't know if he and Kyle could truly be together, but he'd never find another mate. Shifters had one, and when they lost them, they didn't get a second chance. Was Everly ready to lose that because of other people?

He might not have a choice. If someone found him, he'd have to decide whether to stay in Rosewood and stand his ground, possibly pulling the pack into his fight, or run. In the past, he wouldn't even have thought about it. He'd have run, and he wouldn't have looked back.

That wouldn't be possible now. Even if he had to leave, he'd never forget Rosewood and Kyle. He truly wanted to make things work with Kyle, but he didn't feel he could be serious about it until he was sure the pack was as safe as possible.

But it was time to take a break. Kyle would be done with work soon, which meant he'd be home for dinner. Everly wasn't a great cook, but there were a few things he was good at, and he wanted to show Kyle how much he appreciated his mate giving him time and space to think about everything. He understood how hard it had to be for Kyle not to even ask a question about them being mates.

Everly left his computer in the guest bedroom he was using as an office. He was anxious when he was away from it, but he wouldn't have to run like he had every other time. Even if someone got to the pack, Everly wouldn't face them alone, not this time. The thought was both unsettling and made his chest ache in happiness.

He was in the kitchen putting the lasagna in the oven when someone knocked on the door. Kyle never did, so Everly had no idea who it was, but he suspected it was one of Kyle's siblings. All three had visited after Kyle had moved in with Everly, and they were nice. Everly also liked Kyle's niece, a cute little girl with brown hair, a wide smile, and glittering eyes.

Everly wasn't afraid or worried when he went to open the door, still drying his hands. There was another knock, telling him that whoever was there was impatient. Maybe they weren't here for Kyle. It might be someone who was here to see Everly. Everly had been making friends, or at least, he liked to think he was.

He threw open the door, blinking when he found himself face to face with the woman who'd been glaring at him every time she saw him around pack territory. He probably should have asked someone who she was, but he'd dismissed her. She wasn't a danger, and besides, he spent most of his days at home or the gym, so it wasn't like he saw her often.

He looked around, wondering if maybe she had the wrong

house, although he doubted that was the case. "Can I help you?" he asked.

"I'm here for my son," she said.

Everly frowned. "I'm sorry, but I'm not sure what you're talking about."

"I know you're not sorry. You took my son away from me, and I want him back."

Everly still had no idea what she was talking about, but he could imagine. Kyle had warned him that he and his mother weren't talking at the moment and that she was pissed he'd moved out and quit college. Everly never had a family or parents who cared about him, so he thought it was a pity for Kyle to lose his parents this way, but he understood why Kyle didn't want any contact with them.

He understood it even better now that Kyle's mother was standing in front of him.

"You're Kyle's mother," he said.

She nodded curtly. "I'm here to take his things."

Everly stared at her for a moment, wondering if he'd heard that right. Was she saying what he thought she was saying? Did she think he was going to let her in to take her son's things just because she asked? "I'm not sure what you're talking about," he said because he hoped he wouldn't have to fight with her.

Her glare deepened. "It's not hard to understand my words. If you let me in and show me Kyle's bedroom, I'll have everything packed and ready to go soon. You won't have to deal with him for one more second."

"When I opened the door, you accused me of stealing your son, and now you think I'm going to let him go so easily?"

"It would be better for you. You don't want to put yourself against me."

Everly almost laughed. Instead, he bit his lower lip, knowing that laughing in her face would make things worse. It might be funny when he thought about it, but this was still Kyle's mother, and Everly didn't know how Kyle wanted to deal with her.

One thing he *did* know. Kyle had no intention of moving out, and there was no way Everly was letting Kyle's mother in.

"I'm not letting you in," he told her. "I don't care what you say, but Kyle doesn't want to move back in with you. Besides, even if he did want that, I wouldn't let you in unless I talked to him first, and I haven't. He'll be back from work soon, so if you want to talk to him, feel free to wait out here on the porch."

"This is my son's home. I'm allowed in and in his bedroom."

"You're not. Kyle is an adult, and this is *his* home, as well as mine. If you need to talk to him, you're welcome to wait. Otherwise, I have something in the oven, and I need to check on it."

"You're going to regret this."

This time, Everly *did* laugh. Did Kyle's mother think Everly was going to be afraid of her? "Lady, I've faced a lot of dangerous people in my life. I'm a rare shifter, and I've been hunted for as long as I can remember. You're not going to scare me."

Kyle's mother looked like she didn't know what to say. She also looked pissed, and Everly expected her to explode and start yelling at him any second now.

He crossed his arms over his chest. If that was how she wanted to do things, he was ready for her.

Kyle wasn't proud of the fact that he was hiding in the forest, but he had no intention of facing his mother. Besides, Everly was doing a great job of it.

Kyle didn't think anyone had ever talked to his mother that way. He was giddy from how Everly had put her in her place. The only other person who would have dared do something like that beyond Peregrine was Cam, but he was the alpha, and he would have been more diplomatic. Everly didn't seem to care if Kyle's mother hated him, which Kyle supposed was the case. Even if Everly decided to stay, he hadn't struck Kyle as the kind of person who cared what people thought about him.

"I'll tell the alpha how you're behaving," Kyle's mother said.

Her words made Kyle want to bury himself and never come out. Why did she have to humiliate him in front of Everly? He supposed he could have stepped in and told her to leave, but he already knew that if she saw him, the situation would turn out even worse. He had no intention of facing her, at least not right now.

Besides, he'd already told her he was quitting college, moving out, and working for the pack. If she hadn't accepted it the first time he'd told her about it, he doubted she ever would. Would trying to talk to her change anything? He doubted it. He supposed he could try again, but he wasn't in the mood, especially not after the way she was talking to Everly.

"And what do you think the alpha will do?" Everly asked.

"He'll make you leave. This is a good pack, and we don't need you."

"I'm pretty sure Cam thinks differently, but feel free to call him. You can even ask him to come around. I'm sure he'll enjoy my lasagna."

Kyle grinned. This was glorious. He wished he'd thought about recording it with his phone so he could show Marcus. Marcus had had to deal with Kyle's mother since they were children, and he'd never liked her. He would have cheered if he could hear what Everly was saying.

Thankfully, Kyle's mother didn't linger, and she didn't call Cam. Instead, after one last glare at Everly, she huffed, turned around, and stomped off the porch. Kyle stayed where he was, not moving until he was sure she wouldn't see him and that she was far enough away that she wouldn't decide to turn around and yell at Everly some more.

Once she was gone, he stepped out from under the trees. He wasn't surprised to see Everly was waiting for him with the door still open. Everly arched a brow, and Kyle shrugged. "Sorry you had to deal with that," he said as he climbed the porch steps.

"It's fine. I understand why you didn't want to face her."

"She's not easy to deal with."

"She's *awful* to deal with. But she's your mother, so I understand." Everly closed the door. "Still, I don't like the way she tried to take over your life again. You're going to have to talk to her."

Kyle sighed. "I've already tried that, and it doesn't work great."

"Well, she's going to have to understand the situation eventually. Or do you think she'll try to get you to move back in with her until you're fifty?"

Kyle barked out a laugh. "I wouldn't put it past her. It's not like she wants me back because she loves me. She wants back the control she had over me before I left."

Everly nodded. "Well, unless you give it to her, she won't get it back."

God, Kyle was falling for this man, and he didn't know what to do about it. He wanted to blurt it out, but he also didn't want to freak Everly out and send him running.

He might not be able to tell Everly how he felt with words, but maybe he could use his actions. It was a bit corny to think he could let Everly know how he felt through sex, but maybe not. Besides, he wanted to feel close to his mate, and what better way?

"You said you had something in the oven," he started.

Everly smiled. "I'm cooking lasagna for dinner. I hope you like it."

"I'm sure I'll love it, but do we have a little time before it's ready?"

"Sure. Why? Do you want to talk?"

Kyle shook his head and reached for Everly. He didn't want to talk, not right now.

Everly came with a smile, allowing Kyle to pull him closer and kiss him. Kyle felt Everly's entire body relax, as if he'd been waiting for this moment the entire day. Kyle had, and maybe the same went for Everly. Maybe Everly felt like Kyle and didn't know how to say it out loud.

Kyle dropped to his knees. He'd never wanted anyone the way he did Everly, and he wished for Everly to know that. It would have been easier through a conversation, but it would have been messier. This way, Kyle could show his appreciation without putting words on the table.

He looked up, hoping Everly wouldn't push him away. He doubted that would be the case when he saw Everly's expression. His eyes were hooded, and he licked his lips, hungrily looking at Kyle.

Kyle reached for Everly's jeans and popped open the button. He slowly lowered the zipper, and Everly's jeans started slipping down his hips. With just a tug, they fell to Everly's ankles.

For once, Kyle was glad Everly favored too-large jeans instead of skintight ones.

Everly's boxer briefs were the next to go, and when they dropped to Everly's feet, too, Kyle took in his mate. Everly was hard, his cock jutting up from a nest of dark hair. The trail went up, disappearing under Everly's t-shirt. Kyle couldn't wait to see Everly naked, but for now, this would have to do.

He leaned forward and kissed the head of Everly's cock. Everly shuddered but didn't push Kyle away, so Kyle wrapped his lips around his mate's cock.

As he sucked, he reached down for his own pants. His cock was so hard it was almost painful, and he sighed in relief when he was finally able to free it. He wrapped his hand around it as he continued lavishing Everly's cock with attention and started jacking himself off. He wanted to take care of Everly and show him how much he cared, but he also wanted to get off.

As he moved both his mouth and his hand, he looked up. Everly's cheeks were flushed and his lips red where he kept biting them. He reached for Kyle's head, and Kyle nodded eagerly, wanting to feel Everly's hands on him. He didn't even care if Everly was forceful about it. He didn't mind a bit of rough sex, although it had been a while since he'd blown a guy, so he hoped he wouldn't choke on Everly's cock.

But what a way to go if he did.

As he blew Everly, Kyle realized this was one way he could take care of his mate. He enjoyed taking care of people and had wondered if Everly even needed him to. This was the one thing only Kyle could give Everly. He was Everly's mate, and no one else would ever make Everly feel the way he felt now.

And maybe the same went for Everly. Kyle was used to taking care of people instead of having people taking care of him, but that wasn't how relationships worked. That was why some of his relationships had exploded. Kyle didn't want the same to happen with Everly, which meant he needed to allow his mate to take care of him like he wanted to take care of Everly.

Kyle sucked harder and used his free hand on Everly's balls. He rolled them between his fingers, then tentatively pushed one fingertip behind them, searching for Everly's hole.

Everly didn't push him away, so Kyle stroked his finger against it. Everly's hands tightened in Kyle's hair, and he thrust his hips forward, pushing his cock into Kyle's mouth. Kyle relaxed his jaw, his hand flying on his own cock. He felt like he barely needed the stimulation, anyway, because it was satisfying enough to give Everly pleasure.

Kyle kept it up, even when Everly grabbed his face with both his hands and kept him in place so he could fuck his mouth. Saliva dripped down Kyle's chin, and he was pretty sure he would feel this for the rest of the evening, but he didn't care. A little jaw ache was worth it.

Everly groaned and shuddered, and Kyle could tell he'd be coming soon. He stayed where he was, suckling on the head of Everly's cock as it twitched and jerked on his tongue. Kyle eagerly drank Everly down, happy to find out what Everly tasted like.

Everly slumped against the closest wall and let go of Kyle's face. Kyle furiously jerked off until he finally came, his cum splattering on the floor. Both of them stayed where they were for a while, panting heavily. Kyle's knees hurt, but he didn't think he could move.

He let go of his cock and looked down at the floor, grimacing. "I'm not looking forward to cleaning this if it gets dry."

Everly laughed. "Then maybe you should get up and clean it now." He offered Kyle a hand. "Come on. We both need to clean up, and I have to check on the lasagna."

Kyle had expected to be dismissed as soon as he was on his feet, but Everly pulled him into his arms and kissed him. He didn't seem to have a problem with Kyle's mouth tasting like his cock and cum.

They lazily kissed for a moment before Everly let go. He kissed Kyle's nose, causing Kyle to blink. He didn't think anyone had ever done that.

"Come on. We both need to wash up before dinner, and

you also have to clean the floor."

Kyle groaned. "Dammit. Next time, I'm coming in your mouth."

Everly grinned. "I'm counting on it."

CHAPTER FIVE

Everly felt like an idiot, but he couldn't stop smiling. Even something boring like shopping for new boots felt exciting. Being able to have more than a few changes of clothes was something he wasn't used to, just like having a dresser to put those clothes in and knowing he wouldn't have to abandon them when he ran.

He'd made do with the few clothes he had, but he'd been in Rosewood a few weeks now, and he couldn't continue like that. He was still hesitant about staying, even though he could see himself doing just that. Things with Kyle were going great. Pack territory was fenced in, and Everly had placed all the cameras. He was training one of Kyle's friends, Marcus, to keep an eye on the cameras and work them and the program. He and other guards would take turns in the surveillance room so there would always be someone to keep an eye on pack territory.

And Everly had friends. He liked Bryson and Cam, and Arvin had come to visit. He'd also met Arvin's grandson, Owen, and the other rare shifters who called Rosewood home.

All in all, Everly had started to feel at home in Rosewood, no matter how incredible it was. Had he finally found his place in the world? It sure felt like it, and he hoped it would be. He didn't want to leave, not with everything he stood to lose if he did. It wasn't only Kyle, although Kyle was a huge part of that.

Everly grinned like a fool as he walked into one of the

shops to buy new shoes.

Things with Kyle were going much better than Everly could have imagined. Kyle was a sweet man, and while it was obvious he didn't quite know how to behave around Everly, he was trying hard. He wanted Everly to feel at home, and Everly was starting to. He could see himself staying in the long run, for years and possibly decades. He could see him and Kyle being together for just as long, and while it wasn't something he'd ever considered before, he did now. Maybe it was because Kyle was his mate and made what Everly felt for him special. Maybe it was because *Rosewood* was special, along with the people who lived here.

Everly smiled the entire time he spent trying on his new boots and paying for them. He was pretty sure the woman at the checkout thought he was a bit nuts, but he didn't care, and he beamed at her as he paid.

Once he was outside, he tilted his face up to the sky. Yes, this was his home now, and he was never leaving. Everly wanted to stay, and he was going to.

He hadn't told anyone yet, but he wanted to make it special for Kyle. Everly knew that Kyle had been worried he'd get hurt, opening up to him. It made sense. Everly had been on the run most of his life, never staying long in one place. Why would Kyle think the situation was different this time? Yes, Kyle was Everly's mate, but if Everly was in danger, he might not be able to stay. Kyle knew that, and he hadn't demanded anything from Everly. Everly was grateful, but it also bothered him because of all the people in Everly's life, Kyle was the one person who *should* demand things from Everly.

Maybe it was time for them to talk, both about their relationship and their future. For once, Everly couldn't wait. It didn't scare him anymore. Kyle cared about him, and he cared about Kyle. They'd make things work. Everly would make sure of it.

He walked down the sidewalk, wondering what he could put together for tonight. Kyle was usually tired but excited when he came home from work, and hopefully, tonight wouldn't be any different. Everly could get dinner ready, maybe add a few candles on the table and draw a bath so Kyle could clean up when he got home.

Something wrapped around Everly's throat as he walked past an alley. He made a strangled sound and tried to pull away, but what felt like the barrel of a gun touched his back. He froze, wishing he could shift but knowing he couldn't, not in the middle of the day and the middle of town. Some humans in Rosewood might be aware that something was up with the Rosewood pack members and that shifters existed, but it still wouldn't do for Everly to expose the pack and every single shifter in the world.

"Good man," the man who'd grabbed him said. "Go in that alley."

Panic gripped Everly's chest, and his griffin stirred. It wanted out, but no matter how much Everly wished to allow it, he couldn't. He couldn't risk the pack and its safety. Hopefully, the man who'd grabbed him only wanted him. If Everly went with him, he'd leave the pack alone, or at least, Everly hoped so.

He walked slowly. The man's arm was still wrapped around his throat, and he used his hold to steer Everly. Everly looked back, hoping someone had noticed, but no one came after him. No one asked what was going on or if they could help.

Everly was alone, just like every other time he'd been hunted.

But this time, he had someone to protect. If he'd been in this situation before, he would have shifted, not caring about who saw him and what happened. It would have been the only way for him to get away. Now, he couldn't, at least not until they were out of sight, which was going to happen soon. The alley wasn't long, but it would shield him enough that he could shift, beat the hell out of this guy, and fly away.

Something stung Everly's arm. He dropped the bag with the boots and tried to raise a hand, but the guy holding him squeezed his arm around his throat. The gun wasn't at Everly's back anymore, but with the guy still half strangling him, Everly doubted he could do anything.

"What do you want from me?" he asked.

"You know what we want."

Unfortunately, Everly did. It would be no use for him to offer this man anything. It wouldn't be enough. He was worth too much on the black market, and he didn't have enough money to offer to make up for that. He could beg, but he doubted it would make any difference. The only thing he could do to get out of the situation was to run, but how? Maybe he'd be lucky when they reached the van he'd just noticed at the end of the alley. Maybe he'd be able to sneak away then.

He stumbled. His legs felt rubbery, and he didn't understand why. The man had to hold him up, and he finally let go of Everly's throat. Everly tried to take advantage of it and pushed himself forward, but he didn't get far before he stumbled and fell on his knees. Once he was there, he tried to crawl away, which made the man behind him laugh.

"You won't get far, so you might as well stop," the man said as he crouched next to Everly. "Don't make this more difficult than it has to be. Come on, get into the van."

Everly shook his head. "I'm not going to make this easy for you." His words were slurred, and he remembered the prick on his arm. Had this guy drugged him? It would make sense. Many humans didn't want to have to deal with a shifter who wasn't drugged, especially one as dangerous as Everly.

If Everly *had* been drugged, there would be no getting out

of this situation. He wasn't going anywhere unless someone helped him, but no one would.

No one ever did.

The van's side door opened, and another man hopped out. "Are you done playing with him?" he asked.

"Help me get him inside. The sooner we're out of here, the better it will be. Some of his friends might come looking for him."

The new guy grabbed one side of Everly, the one who'd drugged Everly the other. Together, they hauled Everly into the van, no matter how hard Everly tried to fight.

It wasn't enough. He flopped on the floor, curling into a corner. One of the men said something, and the van door slammed closed. Everly closed his eyes. He felt like if he moved, he'd throw up, which was probably the case. He was tempted to do just that to bother these two, but he didn't want to be dehydrated. He was going to fight his way out of this, just like he always did. That meant he needed to keep his energy up and make sure he was strong enough to fight when the time for him to do it came.

Kyle bounced on the balls of his feet as he walked home. He always did these days, and he almost couldn't believe how much his life had changed. Before, he hadn't wanted to go home to his parents, not even when he was on break from college. The less time he spent with them, the better it was for his mental health. Now, things were completely different, and he couldn't wait to go home once he was done working.

Of course, this home was different. He wasn't with his parents anymore, but with Everly, and that changed everything.

Everly changed everything.

Kyle still couldn't believe he'd found his mate and that Everly was so perfect. Kyle knew no one was, not even Everly, with his habit of having the entire house clean as a pin and so neat it looked like no one lived there. Kyle understood it probably came from having to be ready to run at any moment, and hopefully, it was a habit Everly would slowly lose over the years. Kyle wanted Everly to feel at home in the Rosewood pack, and he was doing everything he could to make that happen.

He opened their front door and called out, "Honey? I'm home."

He grinned as he closed the door and started untying his boots. He couldn't hear Everly, who was probably in his office, working on his computer. He took pack security seriously, and while Kyle didn't understand half of what Everly did on his computer, he was glad the pack had him. The place had never been so safe, which meant that the rare shifters in Kyle's life could truly relax now. Even if someone found them, they wouldn't be able to get into pack territory.

"Everly?" Kyle called out as he climbed the stairs.

He couldn't hear the sound of Everly typing on his keyboard, but that didn't mean anything. A few times, he'd come home to find Everly staring at the camera feeds. They now surrounded pack territory, and while it felt a bit much, it was for everyone's safety. Times were changing, and shifters needed to protect their own, even if they weren't the same kind of shifters. Peregrine, Owen, and all the other rare shifters were part of the pack, which made them family, and Kyle wanted to protect them.

He knocked before opening the door of Everly's office. He stepped inside, knowing he'd find Everly there, but the room was empty.

Kyle frowned. "Everly?" he called out again.

No one answered.

He checked all the rooms upstairs, then made his way back downstairs and into the kitchen. That was when he saw the note on the table.

I need new boots. I'll be back soon.

Everly had put the date and time he'd written the note on top, so Kyle knew he'd been gone four hours. It didn't take four hours to go into town and buy a pair of boots, but maybe Everly had gotten distracted.

Unease prickled at the back of Kyle's neck. He felt something was wrong, but it was probably just an impression. He wasn't Everly's keeper, and no matter how anxious he was, he had to believe everything would be okay and that Everly had just gotten sidetracked. Maybe he needed more stuff, or perhaps he'd met someone and was getting coffee. There was no way for Kyle to know but to call Everly's phone, so he tried doing just that.

It went straight to voicemail.

Kyle licked his lips. He didn't want to be the person who freaked out when their significant other wasn't home, but this didn't feel right. Everly was always available on the phone. He'd explained it was because many rare shifters had his number, and he needed to be available in case something happened. If one of them needed help, they just had to call, and Everly did everything he could to get them that help.

But now, his phone was off.

Kyle decided to wait a bit longer, just in case Everly was coming home. It was almost dinner time, and he'd never missed dinner. Kyle wanted to get something ready, but he was too nervous, and instead, he found himself pacing the kitchen and peering out the window every so often to check if Everly was coming back.

He didn't.

After an hour passed, Kyle was sure something had happened. He took his phone out of his pocket as he left the house and dialed Cam's number. Just like Everly, Cam's phone was always on. He was the alpha, and a pack member might need him at any moment. He answered after only a few rings, and while Everly felt a bit guilty because he could hear Toby's voice in the background, this was too important.

"Have you seen Everly?" he asked.

There was a pause, then Cam said, "Hello to you, too, Kyle."

Kyle huffed. "Yes, hello. Have you seen Everly? Because I went home after work, and he wasn't there. There's a note in the kitchen that said he went to buy new boots, but that was more than five hours ago. I know it's still early, but I think something's wrong."

The teasing was gone from Cam's voice when he next answered. "Are you coming over?"

"I am."

The pack had never needed the fence and the cameras, so all the screens that showed the feeds from pack territory were stuffed into one of the guest rooms of Cam's house. He was planning on expanding the gym and adding offices and a security room, but at the moment, this was enough.

"Good. Go to Bryson's house first. He might have news."

"He was working with me."

"It doesn't mean Everly didn't text or call him. Stay calm, Kyle. I know it feels impossible, but it's the only way to help Everly."

Kyle sucked in a breath. Cam was right, and he knew it. He needed to keep his head straight on his shoulders and focus if he wanted to find Everly. What would he do if this was anyone else? What if it wasn't Everly who'd gone missing but another pack member? What would Kyle do, then?

He'd check in with all of Everly's friends. Besides, Bryson's house was on the way to Cam's. It wouldn't take long for Kyle to knock on his door and check in with him.

"I'll go to Bryson's house and ask him if he knows where Everly is," Kyle said.

He already knew Bryson wouldn't. He didn't know how,

but he could tell something had happened to Everly, and he needed to move fast before the people who'd grabbed him got him out of town.

"Good. Bring my brother with you when you come to my house. He'll want to be involved."

"Thank you."

"You don't have to thank me, Kyle. Everly is part of our pack. He's one of us, and we'll do everything we can to find him."

Kyle was touched. It would have been easy for Cam to decide he didn't want his pack to be in trouble and to refuse Arvin's request to give Everly a place to stay when he'd been on the run. Instead, Cam had opened the pack to Everly and to so many other people who needed them. It might have put the pack in danger, but it was nothing compared to the threat Everly and the other rare shifters had to live with every day of their lives.

They hung up, and Kyle ran the rest of the way to Bryson's house. He was glad he hadn't wasted time taking a shower, because he'd need another one soon.

He knocked on Bryson's door, trying to listen in and praying Everly was there. Bryson was alone when he opened the door, though. He was still drying his hair and looking angry, a sure sign that Kyle had interrupted his shower. The scowl on his face disappeared as soon as he saw Kyle, though.

"What happened?" he asked.

Kyle wasn't surprised he could tell something was wrong. "Is Everly here?"

"No. Why would he be?"

Kyle quickly told Bryson what had happened since they'd seen each other at work. He wasn't surprised when Bryson grabbed his boots and pushed his feet inside without even putting on socks. "Let's go," Bryson ordered.

Kyle nodded. He had to remember that he and Everly

weren't alone. If Everly had been taken, they'd get him back.
They had to.

The van stopped, sending Everly rolling to his side. Everly grunted, but that was all he could do. They hadn't been driving long, possibly around fifteen or twenty minutes, which meant they were still close to Rosewood.

Hopefully, close enough that Kyle and the rest of the pack would be able to get to Everly before he was taken away.

Everly knew this was only one stop before he was moved again. He didn't know where they'd taken him, but he didn't need to in order to be aware of what would be done to him. He was a rare shifter, and a lot of people wanted him. He didn't have powers like unicorn shifters, but it didn't mean rich people didn't want to stick him in a cage and show him off to their friends.

God, Everly hated them.

The van door opened. Everly tried to sit up, but his stomach roiled, and he dry-heaved, glad he hadn't eaten much at lunch. The man who'd opened the door took a step back until Everly got himself under control. Then he reached for Everly.

Everly needed to do something. He was weak and drugged, but he didn't know when someone would notice he was gone. Even if they did notice he was gone, would they think it was because he'd wanted to? Everly had been on the run for most of his life, and his friends knew it. They might believe he'd decided it was time for him to move on, although hopefully, even if that was the case, they'd realize he'd never leave his things behind. He hadn't had many of them when he'd arrived, but some things, like his computer, he'd never abandon.

Before the man could touch Everly, Everly exploded forward. He stumbled on his own feet and almost dropped to his knees, but he managed to get himself under control. He started shifting, knowing it would be the only way for him to get out of here, but before he could, a hand grabbed his long hair and pulled. He winced and called on his griffin, but he didn't have the opportunity to let it out.

A punch hit him in the stomach, causing him to fold in onto himself. The hand holding his hair pulled his head back, and he blinked his eyes open to see a man sneering down at him. "Don't try anything funny," the man said.

Everly swallowed. "Let me go."

The man finally let go of Everly's hair. Everly's scalp hurt, but next to the pain in his stomach, it was nothing.

"Unfortunately, we can't do that," the man said. "You're going to earn us a lot of money."

"And you're ready to do anything to get your hands on that money, even take my freedom away."

The man didn't seem to care, but then, Everly hadn't expected him to. "Sorry about that," he said before grabbing Everly's arm and pushing him forward.

The other man grabbed Everly as if he were afraid Everly would try to run. Everly was tempted to do just that, and he looked around, curious to find out where he was. He still felt loopy and like he didn't have full control of his body, but he felt better than before, as if the adrenaline of trying to run away had cleared some of the drugs from his system.

"Don't try anything funny," the first man said. "We'll take it out on your friends if you try to escape."

Everly sucked in a breath. Had these people kidnapped more pack members? "Which friends?"

"The ones you live with. You're part of that pack, aren't you?"

"Leave them alone," Everly said through gritted teeth. He wanted to grab this man and pound his face into the cold cement floor.

"We will, as long as you behave. If you run, we'll head to pack territory and grab whoever we find. It won't be the same as having you for my employer, but hopefully, it'll be enough. So, if you don't want your friends to get hurt or killed, you better behave. The same goes for shifting. I don't know what the fuck you turn into, but I don't want to see it."

Everly narrowed his eyes and leaned closer. He sniffed, which seemed to alarm the guy. He took a step back, glared at Everly, and Everly grinned at him.

He expected the punch to the face, but it still hurt.

"You freak," the man muttered. He looked at the other man, who was still holding Everly up. "Tie him up. I don't want him to have the opportunity to run. If he does, you'll pay."

The man looked nervous but nodded. It was clear who was the boss, but Everly doubted this information would be any good for him. It didn't matter who was in charge, just what would happen to him. Still, it might be good to know who gave the orders and who had to obey them.

Everly wasn't giving up on escaping. He was terrified, but he had faith in his security system. Pack territory was safe, so even if these guys tried to go there to hurt someone, they wouldn't get far. There were cameras everywhere, and someone was always watching the feed. There were guards now, too, although knowing that came with its own anxiousness. If someone attacked the pack, Kyle would be one of the first to be sent out to fight. He was a security guard, and he took his job very seriously. Everly was proud of him, but he was also terrified.

What if he tried escaping, and these guys went to pack territory and somehow got their hands on Kyle? What if Kyle got hurt because of Everly?

This time, Everly didn't try to fight as the second guy dragged him. They were in front of what looked like an abandoned apartment building. Everly couldn't remember seeing it anywhere in Rosewood, but he'd passed a few smaller towns on his way into Rosewood, so he could be pretty much anywhere. He had every intention of escaping, though, so he walked as slowly as the guard would allow him to and took everything in.

Almost all of the windows in the building were broken, the shards of glass glistening in the sun. The van was parked at the back of the building in an empty space that might have been a parking lot before. Now, the concrete was broken and peppered with small flowers and grass that had taken the opportunity to grow there. The van was the only vehicle, which Everly hoped meant he'd only have to deal with these two guys.

The guy pushed him inside through a broken door that had been taken off its hinges and was resting against the wall. Everly blinked, then immediately looked around, needing to understand where he was being taken.

The man continued pushing him down the hallway to their left, then through another door. This one was where it should be, and the man closed it behind them. Everly ended up in what probably had once been a bedroom. There was still one nightstand sitting in the corner, but the bed was gone. The air smelled of dust and rot, probably from that weird brown stain on the ceiling.

There was a chair in the middle of the room, and the man gestured at it. "Sit," he ordered.

"You're going to tie me down?" Everly protested.

The man looked at Everly like he was stupid. Everly had heard the order, too, after all.

"What if I have to go to the bathroom?" Everly asked.

The man shrugged. "Not my problem."

"It's going to be a problem when you have to transport me again."

The man wrinkled his nose. "Sit," he said again, and this time, Everly obeyed.

Hopefully, He'd given the man something to think about, though.

The man quickly tied Everly to the chair, then left the room. He closed and locked it, and Everly wasn't surprised to see that the window was intact in this room. It was locked, but it wouldn't be a problem for him to shift and get out through the glass.

First, he'd have to get untied.

As he went to work on that, he reminded himself that the others were coming. He'd planned for a situation like this his entire life, and when he'd arrived in Rosewood, he'd told Cam about it. He'd wanted Cam to know what to do if something happened to him, and now, something had.

Cam would know where to find him because Everly had told him about the microchip he'd inserted in his own arm a few years ago. He'd come for him—Everly had no doubt about that. He just didn't know if Cam would be in time or if it would already be too late for him.

By the time Kyle and Bryson reached Cam's house, Kyle was frantic. He needed to do something, but he had no idea what. He'd never been in this kind of situation, and he hoped he never would be again. Knowing that someone had taken Everly was awful, especially since Kyle couldn't do anything about it. He wanted to go out there, find Everly and take him home, but how would he find him?

Kyle had just started working as a guard. He had no idea what he was doing or how to find Everly, which meant he'd have to trust his alpha.

Cam would find Everly. Cam would know what to do.

He had to.

When Kyle and Bryson walked in without knocking, the house was already a mess of people. Everyone seemed to be going to Cam's office, so that was where Kyle and Bryson headed, too. There were other guards, along with Cam's beta, Griffin, Toby—Cam's mate—and Sam, Toby's brother. The twins were there, too, one of them looking like he wanted to kill something, while the other bounced on the balls of his feet.

There was no doubt in Kyle's mind who Lennox was and who Carey was, even though he normally couldn't recognize them at first glance.

Cam looked up and gave Kyle a tight smile. "You're here. Good."

Kyle nodded. "Do we know what happened?"

"I don't know anything other than what you told me. We checked the pack cameras, and while we were able to see Everly drive out of pack territory, he never returned. That means he's still in town."

Unless someone had taken him—Kyle couldn't think about that, though. He'd started freaking out, and Everly needed him to keep his head on straight and focus on getting him back instead of panicking.

"Can you tell us what happened?" Cam asked, his voice gentler.

Kyle swallowed. He wanted to go home and act as if nothing had happened, but he couldn't. Everly was gone, and he needed him back. "I have no idea. I went home after work, and he wasn't there. I found a note on the kitchen table that said he needed some new boots and had gone into town. He dated the note and even put what time it was when he wrote it, so I knew it had already been four hours. I waited another hour, even though I knew it wouldn't have taken him that long to buy a pair of boots. When he still didn't come back, I tried calling him, but it went straight to voicemail."

Cam nodded as if he understood how crucial that detail was. "And Bryson hasn't seen him?" he asked, turning his attention to Bryson.

"I was at work with Kyle, so no," Bryson said. "You called Arvin?"

"I already told him what happened. He's coming, but it's going to take him a bit."

"We can't just stay here and wait," Kyle snapped. He sucked in a breath. He'd never spoken to his alpha that way, and while he knew Cam was a good person and would understand, he still didn't like it. "I'm sorry." He and Everly hadn't talked about telling other people they were mates, but he thought it would be better so Cam and everyone else could understand how anxious Kyle was. "He's my mate," he said in a whisper.

Bryson gasped, but Cam just nodded. "I imagined that was the case, but even if it hadn't been, he's important to you. We're going to do everything we can to get him back, I promise."

Kyle could only nod. "How will we find him?"

To his surprise, Cam grinned. "We'll find him, thanks to him."

That didn't make sense.

"What are you talking about?" Bryson asked.

"See, when Everly arrived, he told me something. He knew that one day he'd get caught, and he wanted to be prepared. He injected himself with a microchip."

"So you know where he is," Kyle said.

"I located him, yes. I'm keeping an eye on his location, just in case he's moved, but so far, he hasn't been."

"What are we waiting for?" Kyle asked. He was ready to go out right now and get his mate back.

Cam put a hand on Kyle's wrist. "I want to get him back as much as you do, but there aren't enough of us. I might know where Everly is, but I have no idea how many people are with him. I also can't take all the guards with us. This could be just a ploy to get the guards to leave pack territory and snatch all the rare shifters who live here."

Kyle understood that, but he needed to get to Everly. "How are we going to do this, then?" He was ready to go on his own, although he doubted Cam would allow that.

"Arvin isn't the only one I contacted. I also called the Wakefield pack."

Kyle stared. He'd known Cam was talking to the Wakefield pack. They'd realized they couldn't protect all the rare shifters on their own, which meant they needed help from a bigger pack that had more manpower. "You trust them to help us with this?"

Cam grimaced. "I don't have a choice. Their alpha seems like a good person, though. I've talked to her several times, and she didn't hesitate to offer her people to help us get Everly back. They should arrive here at the same time as Arvin, but she's already put one of her people on it. He's hacking the security cameras all over town."

"That's illegal," Bryson said gruffly.

"It is, but I don't care. I want to know what happened to Everly. We can't move otherwise."

Just then, Cam's phone rang. Cam snatched it from his desk, looked at the screen, and answered, putting the call on speaker. "Angela," he said.

Kyle frowned and looked at Bryson, trying to understand who Angela was, but Bryson shrugged and shook his head, telling Kyle he didn't know, either. Kyle hoped to understand through the conversation, so he listened.

"Your man was kidnapped," the woman said. "I have video of him being pulled into an alley by a guy who's holding him around the throat."

"Can you send me the video?"

"It's already on its way to your email. I'm not sure where your man was taken, though. The guy who grabbed him dragged him into an alley, and we weren't able to find cameras on the other side."

"That won't be a problem. How long until you're here?"

"About half an hour."

"I'm going to send you the location where Everly is being kept. Can your guy check if there are cameras around there? We really should know how many people have him."

"Send everything over to me. We'll find your guy."

"Thank you, Angela."

"You would have done the same if I'd needed your help."

"I would have, but my pack doesn't have the resources yours has."

Kyle had suspected Angela was the Wakefield pack alpha, but now he had confirmation.

She sounded nice, and she was helping find Everly. That was all that mattered to Kyle, but he was glad the other alpha seemed to be a good person. The Rosewood pack was trying hard to protect its members, but Cam was right. They didn't have as many resources as a big pack, which might eventually be a problem.

It had in this case.

"That doesn't matter. What matters is the friendship between our packs, and I'll be happy to have a meeting with you once this is over. It'll be nicer than talking to you on the phone or through a screen," Angela said.

"I'll be happy to talk to you."

They hung up soon after that, and Kyle started pacing the room.

It was good that the Wakefield pack and Owen's grandfather were helping, but it still felt like they weren't moving fast enough. What if the people who had taken Everly moved him? Everly was microchipped, but that didn't mean someone wouldn't notice. What would happen if his kidnappers did?

Kyle had to focus on the positives, but for now, he couldn't see any. He wanted his mate back, and he wanted it to happen now. Unfortunately for him, he wasn't the one giving orders, which was probably a good thing, anyway. He wasn't in his right mind, and he didn't think he'd do a good job. He knew what he was supposed to do as a guard, but this was his mate. All of his training had flown right out the window as soon as he'd realized Everly had been taken, and the only thing Kyle could think of was what would happen to Everly if they didn't get him back.

CHAPTER SIX

Everly should have seen this coming. He'd known people were after him, but he'd felt safe with the pack, and he'd become complacent, so much so that he hadn't been careful while he was in town. This was the result, and he only had himself to berate for that.

He tugged on his wrists, hoping the guy who'd tied him up hadn't done a good job of it, but the ties were tight. His fingertips tingled, a sure sign they weren't getting enough blood. He wasn't in pain, but he would be once the ties were off, which he wasn't looking forward to.

He tilted his head and looked at the ceiling. Knowing this was his fault didn't make it easier to deal with. He'd been distracted, but obsessing over what he should or shouldn't have done wouldn't help. He should be focusing on trying to get the ties off and getting out of his room, which wasn't one of the easiest things he'd ever done.

He cocked his head, thinking he heard footsteps. He wasn't sure, so he continued listening until he was. Someone was coming, and he doubted it was a good thing, at least not for him. He had a microchip, but it wouldn't help if these guys continued moving him.

The door creaked open, and the guy who'd tied him up stepped in. He was holding a bottle of water, which gave Everly pause.

"I'm not drinking that," he said.

"Why not?" the guy asked as if offended.

"Because you won't let me go to the bathroom. You said so

yourself."

The guy frowned. "Aren't you thirsty?"

"I am, but I don't want to pee myself." Maybe Everly could make friends with this guy, or at least, be friendly enough that the guy would let him go. He didn't seem as harsh as the one who'd grabbed Everly and had drugged him before hitting him when Everly had tried to escape. This guy had still helped kidnap Everly, but he was Everly's only chance.

"I'll drink it if you let me go to the bathroom," he tried to compromise.

The guy hesitated. "I can't untie you."

"Does that mean you'll volunteer to clean up when I pee myself?"

The guy grimaced. "This is *not* what I signed up for."

"What did you sign up for? Kidnapping a guy who was minding his own business?"

The guy's cheeks flushed, and he looked away. "It's none of your business."

"Considering I'm that guy, I feel like it is. Why don't you let me go?"

"Because I don't want to die."

Everly stared at the guy, trying to understand him. He didn't seem as eager as the other one to have gotten his hands on Everly, so maybe there was something there. He'd helped kidnap Everly, but it didn't mean he was into this. "They threatened you?"

"I'm sorry. I can't help you."

Everly took the guy in. His dark hair was messy and needed to be washed, and there was a bruise yellowing on the guy's jaw. Someone had beaten him, and while Everly couldn't tell when or why that happened, he suspected the other kidnapper had something to do with it. It would explain why this one was so afraid and why he was ready to kidnap someone to get out of trouble. It didn't help Everly at the moment, but if he had the time, he was pretty sure he could convince this guy to let him go.

The problem was that he doubted he'd have time.

"What's your name?" Everly asked softly.

The guy looked like he didn't want to answer, so Everly was surprised when he eventually did. "Doyle."

"I'm Everly."

"And you're a shifter."

"I am. Are you human?"

Doyle nodded.

That explained why they'd tied up Everly. They were probably afraid he'd shift and attack them, and they wouldn't be wrong. Everly had every intention of doing just that if he had the opportunity, but he didn't want to hurt Doyle if he didn't absolutely have to. Doyle didn't seem like a bad person, just someone who'd ended up in a bad situation. Everly wouldn't hesitate if the only way for him to get out was to hurt Doyle, but it wasn't necessary just yet.

"How did you end up in this situation?" he asked.

Doyle swallowed so loudly that Everly could hear it. "I needed money." Doyle snapped his mouth shut. "You want this water or not?"

Everly sighed. "I'm thirsty, but I also need to use the bathroom."

Doyle eyed Everly as if he didn't trust him, and he probably didn't. "Are you going to try to run away if I let you go to the bathroom?"

"I promise you I won't." And Everly wouldn't, but he hoped that if Doyle had to untie him, then tie him up again, whatever he'd used around his wrists would be looser next time.

Doyle still didn't look convinced, but he came closer. Everly stayed as still as he could, not wanting to spook the human. He was tempted to shift as soon as his hands were free, but he'd made a promise. Instead of escaping, Everly allowed Doyle to guide him toward the bathroom. It was just next door, but Doyle kept looking around as if he expected someone to find them. He probably did, and he knew it wouldn't be good for him if it happened. Whatever the guy who'd kidnapped Everly had on Doyle, Doyle was terrified of him. He was still guilty of helping the guy kidnapping Everly, but Everly understood being in dire situations. It didn't look like Doyle had any say in what he was doing, and it endeared him to Everly.

Just not enough for Everly to care about what would happen to Doyle when all of this was over.

Once Everly was done in the bathroom, Doyle marched him back to his chair. This time, when he offered Everly the bottle, Everly took it. He drank half of the water in one go, then took a small break.

"Thank you," he murmured.

Doyle shrugged as if what he was doing wasn't a big deal. "I don't think this is right," he said.

"Then why are you doing it?"

"Because I have no choice."

"You always have a choice. We all do."

Doyle hesitated, then shook his head. "Not in this case. I wish I had a choice, and I hate myself for this, but I have to do it." He licked his lips. "Sit. I have to tie you up again."

Everly had promised he wouldn't try to run, so he didn't. He drank the rest of the water, handed Doyle the empty bottle, and sat in his chair. He felt more like himself this time, with the drugs gone from his body, and he made sure to keep his wrists just a tiny bit apart so he'd have more leeway when he tried getting the ties off.

Either Doyle didn't notice, or he wanted Everly to escape as much as Everly did. He didn't say anything about it, just tied Everly again and left without another word. Everly watched him go, wondering what the other guy had on Doyle. It was obvious he was using something against him, but what? The most obvious explanation would be that the guy who'd kidnapped Everly had also taken someone who was dear to Doyle, but maybe it was just Everly romanticizing this entire thing. Maybe he just wanted Doyle to be a good guy so much that he projected what he thought had happened to him.

Besides, even if that *was* what had happened, it wouldn't change anything. Everly was getting out of here, and he doubted he'd be able to help Doyle. He would if he had the opportunity, but his main goal was getting out and back to Kyle. Unfortunately for Doyle, that meant he'd be left behind and that he'd have to deal with the outcome on his own.

But Everly had a bit more time left. So far, it didn't look like they were going to move him anytime soon, and he hoped Cam and the others were coming. They had to have realized something had happened to him by now, which meant they were trying to find him. Cam knew how to do that, but it made sense that he hadn't thrown himself and his pack into a rescue mission. He might know where Everly was, but he couldn't know how many people had taken him and what was happening to him.

But he'd come. Everly had faith in the Rosewood pack and the alpha, and he couldn't lose it. He had to remember that he was getting back to Kyle and focus on that instead of everything that could go wrong in this situation.

Kyle didn't like leaving Rosewood. The little town he'd been born in always looked like a paradise when he got a bit further away and saw the towns around it. In Rosewood, everything looked clean and wholesome. A lot of people resented growing up there because nothing ever happened, but Kyle never had. He liked that nothing ever happened in Rosewood, and now that something regularly did, he wished they could get their peace back.

It wasn't just that. The people who lived in Rosewood loved the town and took care of it. There were stores, people who cleaned the streets even when it wasn't their job, and not a lot of crime.

But they weren't in Rosewood anymore. The people who had taken Everly hadn't stuck around. Instead, they took him to a nearby town. Kyle hadn't liked what he saw as soon as they got there, but now he liked it even less.

They parked a bit away from the apartment building in which Cam thought Everly was. They couldn't see much from here, but Kyle didn't need to. He could imagine all too well what the place looked like.

The sight he had from where they'd parked was enough. The apartment building had been abandoned a while ago, and it was in bad shape. The windows were broken, and he was pretty sure he'd seen a pigeon fly in. They had nests there, and Kyle wasn't looking forward to having to go in.

But he would, because that was where Everly was.

"I don't like this place," Marcus grumbled next to Kyle.

"I don't think anyone likes this place."

"True. And we're sure Everly is in there?"

"That's what Cam thinks."

Marcus nodded, his gaze still on the building. "Don't think I won't yell at you for not telling me you've met your mate."

Kyle sighed. He'd expected Marcus to be angry, but he really wished that wasn't the case. "I didn't know if Everly would want me to tell anyone. I didn't even tell my brother or my parents."

Marcus snorted. "Your parents are the last people you tell anything about yourself."

That much was true. "I just wanted to see where things

went. I don't even know if Everly is planning on sticking around. I mean, usually, he's on the move all the time, and he was kidnapped. I don't think he'll want to stay, not when it could happen again."

Marcus finally looked at Kyle. "You can't know that."

"Just like I can't know if he's going to stay. I'm sorry I didn't tell you about him, but I wanted to give us time to get to know each other."

Marcus nodded and clasped Kyle's shoulder. "I get it, and I'm not really angry. I just wish you hadn't had to hide the truth."

"I didn't have to. I chose not to tell anyone because I wanted to give Everly time, and I don't regret it." He never would. Kyle wanted Everly to be comfortable with him. Even more, he wanted Everly to be comfortable in Rosewood. He wanted him to feel safe, and while that didn't look like it might happen after all of this, he still hoped he'd convince Everly to give Rosewood another chance.

"What are we waiting for?" Marcus asked.

"You'd have to ask Cam."

"Maybe we should. It's your mate in there. We have to get to him."

Kyle had never been so happy to have Marcus's friendship. "Cam knows what he's doing."

Kyle looked at the others. Everyone was here—Cam, of course, along with the twins, several members of the Wakefield pack, Arvin, and his grandson, Owen, who was already in his shifted form. He wasn't the only one. Basil, a rare hybrid, had shifted, too, and it took everything Kyle had not to stare at his form.

Cam and the Wakefield pack alpha were talking, and everyone was waiting for their orders. The Wakefield pack alpha had arrived with her hacker, a guy who'd been on his computer the entire time. He didn't even seem to notice the people around him, which Kyle was grateful for. Surely it meant he was focused on helping Everly.

Finally, Cam stepped away from the Wakefield pack alpha and turned toward Kyle. He nodded at him, and Kyle held his breath.

"We're ready to move in," he said. "From what we've been able to find, Everly is being kept in an apartment somewhere on the ground floor. That's all the scouts were able to see, unfortunately. We don't know how many people took Everly, so assume that anyone you meet here is an enemy. I want all of you to be careful, but especially the new members of my security team. I know you want to help, but don't get yourself killed or hurt."

If Cam had been any other alpha, he probably would have left the security team back at home. They were inexperienced, too much so to be here. Kyle was glad he hadn't had to stay back, though. This was the first time he was in this kind of situation, but he'd trained for it, and while he was terrified, he also knew he could do it.

Or at least, he hoped so.

"Kyle, Marcus, you're with the twins," Cam said.

Kyle nodded curtly and walked straight to the twins, sticking closer to Lennox. Carey was grinning like a loon, but then, he usually was. Some phoenixes truly enjoyed going into battle, and Carey was one of them.

"Try not to set anything on fire this time," Lennox said in a dry tone.

His brother rolled his eyes. "What fun would it be if I didn't?"

"We're here to get Everly back, not to burn the entire building to the ground."

Carey pouted. "You're no fun."

"And you're having too much fun."

Before Carey could say anything else, Cam clapped his

hands. "Let's go," he said, and everyone moved.

Kyle and Marcus stuck behind the twins, and Kyle was relieved they'd been paired with them. He might still not know what to think of Carey, but Lennox seemed like a steady kind of guy, and Kyle trusted him to keep all of them safe. He didn't care what Carey decided to do, not even if he burned everything down, as long as they got to Everly and he was fine.

They snuck into the building from what had once been the entrance. One of the doors hung to the side now, looking like someone had tried to tear it off but hadn't managed. There had been a plant in a pot in a corner, but it had died a long time ago, and only a handful of brown leaves were left.

A rat scurried in front of Kyle, and he slapped a hand on his mouth so he wouldn't screech in surprise. Carey looked like he was about to laugh, but he managed to keep himself under control. He patted Kyle's back, then moved forward again.

Lennox and Carey were in the front, with Kyle and Marcus in the back. Kyle was ready to shift at any second if he needed to, but he hoped he wouldn't.

They moved through the building, reaching an open door. Lennox peeked inside, then looked back at the rest of the group and nodded. He stepped in with his brother right behind him.

Someone squeaked, and when Kyle stepped into the apartment, he found Lennox pinning a guy against the wall. The guy's dark hair was all over the place, and his eyes were wide as he stared at Lennox in horror.

Kyle understood why. Lennox looked like he wanted to tear the guy's throat out and wouldn't break a sweat as he did it.

"Where is he?" Lennox asked with a growl.

The guy pointed down the hallway. "In the master

bedroom. I swear, I didn't hurt him."

Lennox frowned, but he finally put the guy down. The guy tried to run, but Lennox grabbed his shoulder and pushed him deeper into the hallway. "Take us there," he ordered.

The guy's legs shook, but he seemed to understand he didn't have a choice. He walked down the hallway, looking as if he expected something scary to jump out from one of the doors they passed at any moment. They reached the one he'd pointed at, and he pushed it open, but he didn't step in. "He's here."

"Is there anyone else inside?" Carey asked.

The guy shook his head. "I'm the only one guarding him."

Carey looked disappointed. "I was looking forward to burning someone, dammit."

Lennox rolled his eyes, grabbed the back of the guy's neck, and pushed him into the room they were standing in front of.

Someone yelled, and Kyle stumbled back when Lennox pushed him. He managed to see into the room for just a second, and he felt like he was going to throw up. Everly was there, but he wasn't alone like this other guy had said. No, he was with the man Kyle had seen kidnap Everly on that video footage. They were in pretty much the same position as on the feed, too. The man was behind Everly with his arm hooked around Everly's throat.

They were too late.

Everly knew something had happened when the guy who'd kidnapped him ran into the room. There were no signs of Doyle, and considering the expression on the asshole's face, Everly wasn't going to like whatever happened next.

The man started to untie him, growled a frustrated sound, and wrapped his arm around Everly's throat, just like he had earlier.

"What's going on?" Everly asked. He sounded calm, but he was anything but.

"Shut up. How did they find us?"

"You realize I have no idea what you're talking about, right?"

But if Everly listened, he could hear people coming closer. The footsteps were unmistakable, and he knew Cam and the others had come for him. He wanted to scream that he was here, but he was afraid of how this guy would react. He was already squeezing Everly's throat hard enough to make it tricky for Everly to breathe.

The door opened, and the arm around Everly's throat tightened even more. Everly sucked in a breath, praying that whatever was happening, he'd come out of it alive. He had too much to go back to and to live for.

Everything was a blur. Kyle appeared at the door, along with other people. Someone pushed Kyle back right away, and he stood there, staring at Everly. Everly wanted to go to him, but the guy holding him in place might have a weapon.

Kyle wasn't alone. The twins were there, and one of them, no doubt Carey, looked gleeful. Everly expected the man holding him to catch fire at any second, and he waited. Carey wasn't as impulsive as Everly expected him to be, though, because nothing happened.

"You're going to let us leave," the man holding Everly said. Something glinted at the corner of Everly's eye, and he sucked in a breath when he realized the asshole was holding a knife to his throat. He'd known the guy was armed, but still.

The other twin, Lennox, raised his hands. "We can't do that. Give us Everly, and you can go wherever you want."

"I don't think so. I'm going to become rich thanks to him, and I'm not giving him up."

Everly wanted to hit the guy. How dare he talk about him this way, as if he wasn't in the room? How dare he act as if

Everly was nothing more than an animal or an object to trade and sell? Everly was so much more, and he didn't deserve to be hunted. He'd finally found a home, and he wouldn't let anyone destroy his happiness, but especially not an asshole like the one holding him down.

He pulled on his wrists, grinning when he realized Doyle hadn't done a good job tying them up. Whether he'd done it on purpose or not didn't matter. The only thing that did was that Everly was pretty sure that as soon as he shifted, the ties would unravel.

It was always tricky to shift in this position—not that Everly had ever been in it. But he'd planned for something like this. And considering his body when he was in his griffin form, he'd hurt himself if he tried shifting while he was tied up. In this situation, though, it should be fairly easy to get free, then turn around and bite the head off of this guy. Everly would have to be fast, because the guy was threatening him with that knife, but he could do it.

He had to.

He wouldn't allow anyone to put themselves in danger because of him, not Kyle, not Lennox, not even Doyle, who was just outside the door, staring with wide eyes. Everly would have left without him if he had to, but as it was, he thought he could help Doyle. He might not deserve it, but maybe he did.

Everly looked at Lennox. Lennox was staring at him as if waiting for Everly to do something. Everly nodded, hoping the asshole holding him wouldn't notice. Lennox nodded back, and Carey's smile widened.

Everly shifted. There was a flash of pain in his shoulder, but it only lasted a moment, and it wasn't so bad that Everly couldn't ignore it. The man holding him shouted and stumbled back, the ties around Everly's arms tore up, and the chair he was sitting on cracked. The clothes he was wearing tore on his growing body, and by the time Everly was on four paws and turned to look at the man who'd kidnapped him, he was in his full griffin form.

He clacked his beak at the guy. The man stumbled back, reaching for the window, but a sudden wall of flame made him move back. He was trapped, and he knew it.

It wasn't enough to stop him. The man screamed and threw himself at Everly without shifting, reinforcing Everly's belief he was human. Everly didn't know what the man thought he'd do with his knife, but he wasn't surprised when the guy tried to stab him. The problem with that idea was that Everly's skin in his griffin form was much thicker than his human one. He also had feathers, and the knife glided over them, not even cutting Everly.

Everly raised a paw and swatted at the guy. He put enough force into it that the guy stumbled and fell down, the back of his head hitting the floor with a sickening crack. He wanted to kill the guy, but he wasn't a killer. He never wished to be one. He just wanted to live his life and never have to worry about being kidnapped or hurt again.

The man tried to get to his feet, but Everly couldn't allow that to happen. He walked closer and pressed his front paws on the man's chest, staring down at him until the man whimpered and the acrid scent of urine filled the air.

"Aw, come on. That's just nasty," Carey complained.

Everly huffed and shook his head. He wasn't surprised the guy was scared. He didn't know what he was playing with when it came to shifters, and hopefully, he'd never be able to hurt another shifter again. Everly didn't want him to even *think* about doing it.

He leaned closer until his beak brushed against the man's nose. The man tried to scramble back, but he wasn't going anywhere with Everly still standing on his chest. Everly growled, making the man close his eyes and turn his head away.

Once he was sure the man was terrified and expected to die any second, Everly stepped away from him.

"I could set him on fire," Carey offered.

Lennox grunted. "You won't set anyone on fire. The entire building would go down with us in it."

Carey pouted. "This is the second fight where I don't get to set anyone on fire. It's not fair."

Everly huffed in laughter. Carey and Lennox would take care of this guy, so he turned his attention to Kyle, who was hovering in the hallway as if he didn't know what to do. His best friend was with him, holding Doyle's arm and looking confused. Everly would have to thank him, too, but first, he needed to deal with Kyle.

He had to have been terrified to come home and not find Everly. Everly could only imagine, and he hoped it wouldn't be enough to push Kyle away. The worst that could have happened had happened. Everly had been kidnapped.

But he'd made it out. His friends had come for him, and they always would, every time he was kidnapped. He hoped it wouldn't happen again, but if it did, they'd deal with it together.

He shifted to his human form, not caring at the way Marcus's eyes widened. Doyle squeaked and closed his eyes, but before Everly could do anything else, Kyle was throwing himself at him.

Everly wrapped his arms around Kyle and held him close. He buried his face into Kyle's hair and took a deep breath, letting his mate's scent help him settle down. He was angry, and he'd been terrified, but all of that was in the past. He was safe, and, more importantly, he was home.

Kyle had hoped they'd find Everly, but he'd been terrified

something would have happened to him.

Something had. Everly had been kidnapped, tied to a chair, and drugged. This situation could have gone a lot worse, and it was a miracle it hadn't. It was a miracle Everly was in Kyle's arms, safe and with only scratches on his body. Kyle wasn't a praying man, but right now, he wanted to fall to his knees and thank whoever had been watching over Everly.

"I'm okay," Everly murmured. He gently stroked Kyle's hair, and Kyle allowed himself to slump harder against his mate. Now that they were together, he could relax and finally allow the fear, panic, and every other emotion that had threatened to take over earlier to do so now. They weren't out of the woods yet, since they were still in the building, but even if there were more men than the two they'd encountered, they were safe because their family was there, fighting for them.

Kyle had been hesitant because he hadn't believed Everly needed him. Now, he knew it had been a flawed assumption. Even though Everly was bigger and better trained than Kyle, he'd always need Kyle. It might not be to free him from kidnappers that were intent on selling him, but this, being wrapped around each other, comforting each other, was something only Kyle *could* do for Everly.

"I'm okay," Everly murmured.

Kyle nodded. "I know."

"I'm also very naked."

Kyle laughed. He'd never have thought he could laugh in this kind of situation, but he was so relieved that Everly was okay that he was afraid he'd start crying instead. His eyes prickled, and his throat felt tight, and it was better if he laughed.

"There's not much left of your clothes," Carey said, poking at what had once been Everly's jeans.

"But some people came prepared," Lennox intervened.

He reached into one of the pockets in his cargo pants and

took out a bundle of fabric. He threw it at Everly, who let go of Kyle to catch it.

Everly looked down, then grinned. "Thanks. I thought I'd have to shift again or walk around naked."

Lennox shook his head. "I know how that feels, and I thought you'd rather have a pair of shorts."

Kyle took a step back to give Everly space to put on the shorts. They were bundled tight and tied with an elastic band, but it only took him a moment to untie it and shake out the fabric. He quickly put them on, gave the remnants of his clothes and shoes a side glance, and took Kyle in his arms again. "I suppose this will have to do."

"What else do you have in there? Oh, do you have a snack?" Carey asked his brother.

Lennox rolled his eyes and ignored him. "The two of you should head outside," he told Everly and Kyle. "Carey and I will take care of these two."

Everly looked at Marcus, who was holding the other guy's arm. "Don't hurt Doyle," he said.

Kyle blinked. "Who's Doyle?"

Everly tilted his chin toward the guy with Marcus. "He tried to help, even though there wasn't much he could do."

As far as Kyle was concerned, Doyle and everyone else who'd helped kidnapped Everly could burn in Carey's flames. His mate was nicer than him.

"These fights are no fun," Carey complained, but thankfully, he didn't try to set anything on fire.

Instead, he turned his attention to the man who'd threatened Everly with the knife. The man's eyes widened, and he tried to crawl away, but Carey placed a boot against the man's back, pushing him into the ground. "Where do you think you're going?" he drawled as he flicked his fingers and flames danced on his hands.

Kyle didn't care. The only thing he cared about was Everly

and taking him home.

Everyone needed protecting sometimes, and right now, that was what Everly needed from Kyle. He'd been through an ordeal, and he needed rest, a shower, and food.

When they stepped out of the building, they found everyone else already gathered outside. Cam was talking to the Wakefield pack alpha, but he looked up when he heard them.

"Glad to see you in one piece," he told Everly.

Everly smiled back. "Glad to see that you came to get me."

"You knew we would. You're one of my pack members, which means you're family. We'll always come for you if you need us."

Everly nodded. "I'm starting to realize that."

"Why don't you and Kyle take one of the trucks? We'll deal with clean-up and get back to pack territory once we're done. I'm sure you want to go home as soon as possible."

"If you're sure you don't need me for anything, I'd be happy to go."

"I'll talk to you tomorrow, once you've had some rest. It's late, and we could all use a good night's sleep."

Things wouldn't always be this way when Kyle went on rescue missions. Cam had allowed him to leave without helping with the clean-up because his mate had been kidnapped, and that was fine. Kyle would deal with everything next time. For now, he'd focus on Everly.

They climbed into the truck Kyle had been in when he and the others had arrived. He looked at the building once before turning on the engine. He'd almost lost his mate in there, and if he could, he'd burn it to the ground. He wasn't a phoenix, which he supposed was a good thing at the moment. He was only a wolf, and his wolf wanted them to focus on their mate.

He drove away as soon as Everly had settled in the passenger seat. He wanted to get Everly as far away from this place as he could.

"Do you need to see the healer?" he asked as he drove.

Everly shook his head. "I promise I'm fine." He reached out and squeezed Kyle's thigh. Kyle took his hand and linked their fingers together, not wanting to let him go.

"I'm taking you home, then?"

Everly sighed and smiled. "Please. I just want to crawl in my bed and not get up for a week."

Kyle was sure they could arrange something like that.

They were silent as he drove them home. He had many questions about what had happened, but it was also good to be this way and bask in his mate's presence without saying anything. Everly would have to answer enough questions tomorrow, and he didn't need them from Kyle, too. Besides, what had happened didn't really matter as long as he was okay.

Kyle relaxed as soon as they crossed into pack territory. One of the security guards at the entrance waved them in, and Kyle waved back, relieved to know that Everly would be safe. No one could get to him as long as he was in pack territory, and while Everly would have to leave eventually, if only to go to the grocery store, for now, he wasn't going anywhere.

Kyle drove to the house he and Everly shared and parked in front of it. He turned off the engine, and both he and Everly stayed silent. Kyle wasn't sure what to say or if there was anything he could or needed to say.

"Let's go inside," Everly murmured.

They climbed out of the truck, and Kyle took a deep breath. Everly was fine. Kyle had to keep that in mind, even though it wasn't easy. He was still panicked when he thought about what happened, and he had to remind himself that Everly was next to him and that nothing would happen to him anytime soon. Kyle would go to the grocery store with him if he had to. He'd protect his mate, and he'd give Everly anything he needed.

Kyle wasn't quite sure what to do now that Everly was home or how to help. He wanted to wrap himself around his mate and never let go, but Everly no doubt wanted a shower and to get into bed.

Right?

They headed inside and stopped at the foot of the stairs. Everly looked like he didn't know what to do, either, which reassured Kyle but also made him feel guilty. Everly needed to focus on himself right now, and so should Kyle.

Kyle shuffled his feet. "You should head upstairs. I'm sure you're tired."

Everly arched a brow but didn't protest. "I could use a shower," he said instead. "That place wasn't exactly sanitary."

"I'll grab a shower, too. I didn't get the chance to when I got home earlier."

Everly's smile was gentle. "I'll see you after our showers, then."

He climbed the stairs, and Kyle watched him go. Everly didn't seem to have a problem walking around nearly naked in front of Kyle, and Kyle couldn't look away. Everly's ass was high and round and perfect, and Kyle wanted to bite it.

Maybe tomorrow.

With a sigh, he followed Everly upstairs. He went to his bedroom, although he wished he weren't staying here anymore. He'd wanted to give Everly time and space, and he was glad he had, but after what had happened, he wanted to spend the night in Everly's arms and reassure himself that Everly was there and that he was okay.

Kyle turned on the water in the shower and stripped, dumping his uniform in the corner of the room. Cam had given him the day off tomorrow, so he'd worry about the mess he was making then. He was exhausted, yet he wasn't sure he'd be able to sleep without Everly in his bed.

Kyle was ready for bed by the time he was done. He dried

his hair as well as he could, not caring if it was damp, wrapped a towel around his waist, and went back to his bedroom.

Everly was sitting on the bed.

Kyle froze, then remembered that Everly had said they'd see each other after their showers. Kyle hadn't expected to be naked when they did, but he doubted Everly cared from the way he stared at Kyle's chest.

Kyle smiled. "I thought you'd already be sleeping. You must be exhausted."

Everly rubbed his chest. He was wearing a pair of pajama pants and nothing else, exposing himself to Kyle's gaze. He didn't seem to mind Kyle looking, so Kyle did without trying to hide it.

They stayed like this for a moment, staring at each other. Kyle's heart raced, and he wondered what Everly would say if he asked him to spend the night. Before he could, Everly got to his feet. Kyle thought he'd leave, but instead, he came closer and gently took one of Kyle's hands.

"Kyle?" he asked softly.

Kyle licked his lips. "Yes?"

Everly pulled him closer, twisting around at the same time. He pushed Kyle toward the bed, and Kyle went, trusting Everly without hesitation. He ended up on his back, looking up at his mate.

When Everly didn't move, Kyle grinned and sat up. He grabbed Everly and reversed their position, unable to look away as Everly ended up on his back under him. Kyle's towel had come undone, but he didn't care.

Everly reached for Kyle's face as Kyle pulled his pajama pants to get them off. "What are you doing?" he asked.

His voice was rough with what Kyle prayed was desire. "What does it look like I'm doing?"

"You don't have to do anything you're not ready for. I

know we haven't talked about the future yet."

Kyle cocked his head. "We've already done this."

"I know, but I hadn't been kidnapped then. I hadn't scared you as badly as I have now."

Everly ran his thumb along Kyle's lower lip. Kyle could have reassured him with his words, but he decided to go another way instead. He tilted his head and caught Everly's thumb between his teeth, pulling it into his mouth. He sucked on it and watched as Everly's eyes widened and his pupils grew bigger.

Kyle let go of Everly's thumb and went back to getting Everly's pajama pants off. This time, Everly helped, pushing his hips up, then raising his feet. Kyle dumped the pants on the side of the bed and leaned down. He closed his eyes, inhaling the scent of Everly's body. He recognized Everly's shower gel, but he wanted more, so he buried his face in the groove between Everly's thigh and his groin. Everly sucked in a breath, but Kyle was focused.

He licked the base of Everly's cock, making his way up the rod. He gently held it up with his fingers, tasting the shower gel he'd smelled seconds ago. Just under it was the taste of Everly's skin, which was what Kyle had been looking for. He sucked in Everly's cock, focusing on the head for a moment, running the tip of his tongue around its ridge, then suckling at it until he felt Everly go rigid under him.

Everly looked at Kyle like he couldn't believe what was happening, and Kyle felt the same. He'd wanted this so much, and now that he had it, it felt like a dream.

But it wasn't. Kyle had Everly back, and he was never letting him go.

Everly raised himself on his elbows, his gaze still on Kyle. Kyle wanted to drive him nuts. He sucked and licked, sometimes used his teeth, making sure Everly enjoyed everything he was doing. He was startled when he felt Everly's fingers on his back, as low as Everly could reach. Kyle had a pretty good idea of what Everly wanted, and he was on board with it.

He twisted his lower body, shuffling on the sheets until Everly could touch his ass. Everly's fingers slipped between Kyle's ass cheeks. They were slick, but Kyle only wasted a few seconds to wonder where Everly had gotten the lube and when he'd used it. He didn't care, not when one of Everly's fingers was pushing into him.

Kyle continued swallowing Everly's cock as Everly fucked him with his fingers. Everly also shallowly thrust up his hips every so often, as if he couldn't stop himself. Kyle liked that. He wanted the tight control Everly always had on himself and his life to unravel, at least when they were alone in bed, in their home.

This house was home. Everly was home.

Everly reached for Kyle's arms and pulled him up. They kissed as Everly rolled them again, and Kyle ended up under him. He opened his legs, ready to welcome his mate into his body and never let go. He wanted more, but Everly had something else in mind. He thrust two fingers into Kyle's ass again, making him whimper. Kyle reached up and grabbed his pillow, twisting his fingers into the cover.

"Ready?" Everly eventually asked.

"I was ready five minutes ago."

Everly rolled his eyes but thankfully also grabbed his cock. He shuffled on his knees until he was close enough and leaned down to kiss Kyle. Kyle kissed him back, pulling him even closer, smiling when the head of Everly's cock brushed against his hole.

He was ready.

Everly pushed in. It had been a while since Kyle had done this, but he remembered how it worked. He relaxed as much as he could and focused on the pleasure that would come as soon as the stinging pain was gone.

He wrapped his arms around Everly's neck, holding on to him as Everly thrust in and out of his body. Everly's lips were slightly open, his long hair all fluffed up around his face, and his pupils blown with pleasure.

Kyle moaned, both from the sensations coursing through his body and from the way Everly looked at him—as if he were the center of Everly's world and all Everly could ever want.

Everly fucked Kyle the way Kyle had wanted since they'd met, and Kyle met him thrust for thrust until he couldn't stand it anymore. He clutched at Everly's shoulders, needing more but feeling like he'd explode if he got it.

Everly pushed his arms under Kyle's thighs, opening him up even more as his rhythm grew faster, as he pushed into Kyle harder and harder. Sweat rolled down his face, and Kyle caught his lips, kissing him as if the world were ending. Everly grabbed one of Kyle's ass cheeks and squeezed almost painfully, causing Kyle to cry out and press his head against his pillow.

The hint of pain was all Kyle needed. He came between them, screwing his eyes shut as he did. Everly continued moving, but not for long. When Kyle felt Everly's cock twitch inside him, he smiled, happy at the knowledge that he'd been the one to give his mate such pleasure.

Everly kissed Kyle, and Kyle opened his eyes. They kissed lazily, and Kyle knew he'd never have enough of this. He'd never have enough of Everly, and if Everly decided it would be safer for him to leave, then Kyle would go with him.

He'd miss his friends and his siblings, but Everly was the center of his world, the man he wanted to spend the rest of his life with. He was never letting him go, no matter what happened.

CHAPTER SEVEN

Everly stalked between the trees, trying to find who he was after. He could hear him, but he couldn't see him. He knew he wasn't far, though, and he'd find him.

A branch cracked in the distance. Everly froze and listened. He would have grinned if he'd been in his human form, but he wasn't, and his beak didn't lend itself to a smile. He crouched, ready to pounce, and waited.

His prey appeared after a few moments. The wolf was looking around, trying to find Everly, but Everly knew this game. He'd played it with people more dangerous than the wolf, and he'd win this time, too.

He waited until the wolf gave him his back—it was a mistake the wolf would regret.

Everly pounced, throwing himself at the wolf. The wolf squeaked and tried to get away, but Everly already had him. He used his wings to trap the wolf close to his body, then he lowered his head and nuzzled the wolf's head.

The wolf huffed, but he leaned back. He rubbed his face against Everly's beak, then down his neck, marking him with his scent. Everly loved that, and he sighed in pleasure as he allowed Kyle to do whatever he wanted to him.

Things had been going well between them. Kyle had been jumpy the first few days after Everly had been kidnapped, clearly afraid someone would try to take Everly again. Everly wanted to reassure him, but he doubted anything could. The only way to show Kyle he'd be okay was to live his life without fear, and that was what Everly was trying to do.

There was still a possibility someone would kidnap him or one of the other rare shifters who lived with the Rosewood pack. That would always be true, as long as people wanted to get their hands on rare shifters and use them. But pack territory was safe, and knowing that made it easier for Everly to breathe and live his life without obsessing. Yes, someone might still try to take him, but Cam and Kyle would find him if it happened. He was sure of that, and that was what had made him decide to stay in Rosewood.

Well, that and his mate, along with the friends Everly had started making. He could imagine a life here, and he didn't want to lose it. Everly had a home for the first time in his life, and he wasn't allowing anyone to run him out of it.

He shifted and wrapped his arms around Kyle's furry body. "We really should go. They'll be waiting for us."

Kyle huffed and settled deeper against Everly's body. It was a sure sign he had no intention of moving, and while Everly agreed, they had a meeting to go to.

Things had been a bit of a mess after Everly had come back. The Rosewood pack had been trying to find out who was behind the kidnapping, as was Everly, but he'd already known he wouldn't find out. Whoever had enough money to hire two guys to kidnap him wouldn't be easy to find, even with Doyle's help.

And he *was* helping. Everly had spoken to him a few times in the past days, and Doyle was truly sorry about his involvement. He'd apologized so much that he was driving Everly nuts, but Everly understood where he was coming from. He'd been forced to do it because he wanted to keep his family safe, and that was something Everly could understand. He'd do anything he had to in order to keep Kyle safe, even kidnapping someone.

Everly rubbed Kyle's fur, grinning when Kyle rolled onto his back to show him his stomach. He gave that area a bit of love, too, but unfortunately, they really didn't have a lot of time. He patted Kyle's thigh, then got to his feet to get his clothes. "Come on. We need to go."

Kyle stayed with his paws in the air for a bit longer, just until Everly was dressed. Then, he shifted, too, and came to get his clothes.

Everly grabbed him before he could, hooking an arm around Kyle's neck and pulling him close for a kiss. He took his time, even though he and Kyle had the meeting to get to.

"I thought we needed to go because we'll be late for the meeting?" Kyle asked, teasing clear in his voice.

Everly smacked Kyle's naked ass. "We will, so put your clothes on."

Kyle grumbled as he did so, and Everly took a moment to take in everything.

This was his life now — being able to shift and run in the forest anytime he wanted, playing around with Kyle, kissing and making love to him. Everly could have never imagined something like this would happen to him, but it had, and it was precious. He'd been given a chance at a life he hadn't thought he'd have.

He and Kyle made their way to Cam's house. They walked in silence, holding hands, and even this simple gesture made Everly smile. He had everything he'd ever wanted with Kyle and the Rosewood pack.

He wasn't surprised to see a car parked in front of Cam's house when they reached it. Cam had mentioned something about the Wakefield pack sending someone to this meeting, and Everly was eager to get to know the person. He'd been surprised to find out the Wakefield pack had helped when he'd been kidnapped, but pleasantly so. Rosewood would need help to protect the rare shifters who lived there, and it seemed like the Wakefield pack was eager to do that. Everly wasn't sure they could trust them yet, but they wouldn't find out by staying away from them. Everyone needed to be involved, which was what was happening right now.

Cam smiled when Everly and Kyle stepped into his office. "We were waiting for you."

Everly smiled apologetically. "It's my fault. I've never had much freedom to shift and play around, and I should have known better than to do that right before the meeting."

Cam chuckled. "It's not a problem. We had a lot to talk about, anyway."

Everly turned his attention to the man sitting on the other side of Cam's desk. He was young, with short blond hair carefully styled and glittering blue eyes. Everly vaguely remembered seeing him when he'd been rescued, but he didn't think he'd ever been told the man's name.

He offered him his hand. "You helped my pack find me. Thank you."

The man shook Everly's hand. "It was a pleasure."

"I wouldn't call it that, not from my point of view."

The man laughed. "I'm Angus."

"Everly."

"I know."

Of course he did. "You'll have to excuse me. I'm not used to dealing with people. I spent most of my life on the run, so I haven't had the time to make friends."

Angus's smile widened. "Not a problem. I look forward to working with you."

Everly blinked. "Working with me?"

Cam cleared his throat. "Angus is the hacker who helped us find you."

Cam had said something about that to Everly, but Everly hadn't given it much thought. Now that he knew who Angus was, he was excited. He had a lot of plans, both when it came to the Rosewood pack and to shifters in general.

"My alpha couldn't be here today, but I'll tell her

everything that'll be said during this meeting," Angus said.

"So, we're listening," Cam said as he sat behind his desk. "Why did you want this meeting?"

"Being kidnapped made me realize that rare shifters need to stop hiding."

Kyle already knew what Everly was planning to say. He squeezed Everly's shoulder from his spot behind Everly. He could have sat, but Everly liked that he was staying close.

Cam and Angus looked confused.

"More rare shifters will be kidnapped if they don't hide," Angus pointed out.

"If we allow things to continue the way they've been going, sure. I think we need to go on the offense."

Cam leaned forward. "What does that mean exactly?"

"Well, I haven't made any definite plans for now. But with the network between the various packs and the rare shifters network in place, I believe it's time to start looking for the people so eager to kidnap me and other rare shifters. There aren't that many people in the world with enough money to pay for us, and if we can hack into their computers and find out their names and where they live, we might be able to strike before they do. At the very least, we could keep an eye on them and make sure they don't get close to us."

"I like that idea," Angus said. He was almost vibrating with excitement.

"And we should continue adding people to both networks. I'm glad the Wakefield pack decided to help us, and I'm sure they're not the only pack around here, or even in the country, who wants to keep the rare shifters safe and are ready to do anything to make that happen. There might not be many shifters around, but we're still a force to be reckoned with."

"This is going to take a lot of planning," Cam said.

"It will, and it won't happen fast, but I still think it's the best thing we can do. Hiding and running haven't helped.

Many rare shifters have disappeared from the network over the years, and we all know it's because they were taken, not because they found a safe place to spend the rest of their lives. I want their freedom and to be able to give them a home, just like Rosewood has with me."

"I'm in," Cam said.

"I'll have to talk to Angela, but I think she'll agree that the Wakefield pack is in, too," Angus said.

Everly grinned. This was just the beginning, and it would be a long road, but they'd make it happen. They'd give every single rare shifter in the country the possibility to live their life safe and happy. That was all Everly had wanted when he'd been on the run, and now that he had it, he wanted every other rare shifter to be able to have it, too.

ABOUT THE AUTHOR

Catherine is the creator of several series, most of them paranormal, including the Whitedell Pride Series and the Gillham Pack Series. While she graduated in translation, she decided to go the writer's way because it was more fun to create her own stories and characters.

She's been living in Italy for more than twenty years, but she's a daughter of the North—Belgium to be precise—and she misses it so much that she's already planning to move back.

She loves pizza—probably too much—her son, her pets, and of course, books. She sneaks some reading time into her schedule every time she has five minutes free from writing, demands from her various pets and son, and lastly, housework.

Connect with her:

lievens.catherine@gmail.com
BookBub: https://www.bookbub.com/authors/catherine-lievens
Website: https://authorcatherinelievens.com/
Facebook: https://www.facebook.com/catherine.lievens.9
Facebook Group: https://www.facebook.com/groups/411788002341528/
Twitter: https://twitter.com/authorCLievens
Newsletter: http://eepurl.com/c-uvKn